# Horty Brown and Co

*A kiss is a window to the heart ...*
*it will give you the answer*

## GARY SEEARY

Front cover photo: Arthur Fox – Boys and girls paddling at Beaumaris Beach (possibly Mentone). Circa 1906.
Back cover photo: Beaumaris Tramway Company horse-drawn tram at Sandringham. Circa 1905. Photographer unknown.
Book and cover design: Luke Harris. Working Type Design @workingtype



First published in 2024 by Gary Seeary Books, Mentone, Victoria, 3194
ISBN: 9780648002864 (novel)
ISBN: 9780648002871 (e-book)
Copyright © Gary Seeary 2024

**GS**



Prepublication Data Service entry is available from the National Library of Australia.
http://catalogue.nla.gov.au
Editor: Deborah Seeary
Typeset in Garamond.
Printed by Lightning Source, Boronia, Australia.

**GARY SEEARY WAS BORN** in the town of Stawell in the Wimmera region of Victoria. He currently lives with his wife, Deborah, in the bayside area of Melbourne.

They have two adult children and six grandchildren.

Gary has written three previous novels, *Sebastian Carmichael*, *The Beautiful Journey*, and *The Moonbeamers*, each reflecting a different era in Australian history.

In his latest novel, Gary features the lives of children from 1900s Mentone. *Horty Brown & Co* is the result.

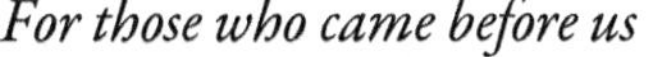

*For those who came before us*

## *Acknowledgements:*

I AM EXTREMELY GRATEFUL to have had the support of so many wonderful people in the production of Horty Brown & Co, which includes my editor Deb Seeary for her intuitive editing and love, our good friend Pete Hobbs for sharing his extensive knowledge of beekeeping.

Chris and Norma Shattock for bringing to light remarkable features of early Beaumaris. Dr Cheryl Threadgold O.A.M. and the Beaumaris U3A for supporting my creative endeavours.

My workmates Wendy, Shane, and Darren for their knowledge and love of horses racing, and an extra nod to Shane for giving me the line, 'I smell a rat.'

Members of the Mentone Public Library for listening to and giving feedback on early chapters. The staff of the Mordialloc and District Historical Society based at the Old Mentone Bakery Museum for their extensive local knowledge.

Graham Whitehead and the late Leo Gamble for their wonderful book: *Mentone Through the Years*. The late Addie Fairlam for her vivid recollections of early life in the bayside area in her book: *Bid Time Return*.

The Kellerman family for their contribution to the early artistic scene in Mentone and district.

Luke Harris for his vision and professionalism in the design of this and my previous books.

(Won't you come home) Bill Bailey: Lyrics and music by Hughie Cannon, 1902.

Pierrots' Ditty: Sung at St Kilda beach by the English Pierrots, circa 1905.

# Twilight at Beaumaris Bay

Between dog and wolf a fire shall rise
To banish the shadows and fog despised
That shelters sheer cliffs and sudden demise
deceiving the moon and beautiful tide

Shells abandoned along the shore
Sing to lovers you will hold no more
Caressed by waves that roll and sway
Entwined forever on Beaumaris Bay

M. Lecrivain

# Part One

# Playing Possum

**Late January 1905**

"Alistair Lundy, whadayuh doin' with your arms in that hollow?"

Horty shouted up to me and then chuckled to herself believing she had taken me by surprise. However, I was well-aware of her approach, as she had cursed while climbing the nearest fence, stepped on every piece of bark as she pushed through scrub, and then trampled on dry bracken as she moved around below.

To distract me further, she then felt the need to poke my backside with a stick while my body was stretched upwards, my feet precariously balanced on a sap covered knot and my arms penetrating deep inside the dark and extensive cavity of a manna gum.

"If yuh tryin' to grab a brushie, Loon – it'll rip yuh!" Horty stated as if an expert on the animal.

"Brushies don't play dead."

Distracted from the minute tugs and prods against the piece of carrot held in my right hand, I looked down upon the impressive spray of freckles on Horty's nose and cheeks, and her big familiar blue eyes peering at me through the midday sun.

Horty's gaze then shifted abruptly in the direction of the bay and something that had attracted her attention at the bottom of Plummer Road. After tying her thick mousey-blonde hair back into a ponytail and then covering it with her favourite straw hat, she turned back to the manna gum and stated with less certainty.

"I don't think ringtails play dead, either."

I wanted to tell her to clear off, but instead held my tongue and waited for her to complete a full pirouette in her pristine white Sunday best before I whispered.

"Can yuh shut your cakehole for one second, Hort? I'm tryin' somethin' Loz Little done a couple a' weeks back."

"Whadayuh tryin' to be like that rat for, Loony Lundy?" Horty said while inspecting the hem at the back of her dress, then grumbled to herself.

"Can't wait to get this scratchy old rag off."

"Well, why don't yuh go home and get yourself changed 'fore yuh new mum catches yuh out here?" I said too soon, realizing I might as well have waved a red rag at a bull.

"Shut yuh gob, Loon! She ain't any sort of mum to me."

A graze to my right hand by the possum's claw drew my attention back inside the manna gum. The nocturnal animal then gave a robust tug and took the carrot from my grip.

At that point, it struck me that perhaps I was relying too much on the scant advice my good friend, Neville 'Sniffle' Schaufelle, had given me after observing renowned trouble-maker Loz Little pluck a brushtail possum from a tree on Charman's old property while urged on by his errant friends from Cheltenham, who of late, had gained a reputation for stealing luggage and harassing passengers in the vicinity of Cheltenham Station.

With no other advice to rely on, and with Horty still scratching the back of my legs trying to urge proceedings along. I had nothing else to do except follow my instincts.

Slowly and gently, I moved the back of my left hand deeper and higher into the hollow until it rested against the animal's silky fur, feeling warmth and the faint beat of a heart. Not wanting to lose any of my gains, I held that position.

"Guess who's comin' Loon?" Horty said and then could be heard kicking the ground. I knew by the disdain in her voice that her father's new wife of five years would soon be passing. I ignored this comment, especially now with my hand poised under the ribs of a wild animal, while also having no desire to add fuel to the dislike Horty already held for Lizbeth, a woman, who could with a push, be her older sister.

"Well, I'll tell yuh if yuh not talkin'," Horty snapped,

although her voice faded as the freshening northerly wind running down Plummer Road carried her words out and over the bay.

"Dad's missus is comin' up the track. The young'un who got her claws into him when he was in mournin' – and can you believe it, she keeps tellin' me the future for a young lady is in the connections she makes in society during her formative years."

The stick stopped scratching my leg and could be heard crashing into a nearby bush.

"All she had to do was be a sneaky, calculating hussy disguised as a prissy lady," Horty said in a high-pitched affected tone.

"And she wants me to be a prissy lady, too," Horty added, her words full of scorn, "Can you imagine me sittin' in the corner of a parlour, lookin' like a stuffed doily?"

I wasn't sure if it was luck or a growing irritation with Horty's attitude, but I lifted the possum in one motion, took hold of its long, fat tail in my right hand and then moved it steadily out of the hollow. Its weight and size substantial, and I'm sure happy with itself, as its home was next to the Browns just budding Jonathan apple orchard, an orchard that Horty's family and mine had tendered to for many years to bring to a point where it was the envy of the neighbourhood or anyone else who found themselves wandering near the slopes of Mentone.

Not wanting to have anything to do with the midday

sun, the possum then dropped the carrot and nuzzled its head deep under my armpit.

"Loon, that's amazin'! – He's a real fatty boom-bah, ain't he, or is he a pregnant she? – Smells like a he!" Horty said with astound while steadying my back as I stretched down to find firm ground, not waiting a second later to smooth the possum's fur.

"Now, I'm standin' back, 'cause it's gonna pee on yuh, for sure," Horty said and then made a strange squeaking noise as she looked back to see Lizbeth's trap dip and roll along an uneven section of Plummer Road.

"Have a bloody look at this, Loon. I think Sniffle's sittin' up next to the missus," Horty added as she grabbed my arm, almost dislodging the possum. "Come over to the rail – Oh, my goodness, Sniffle's got Samuel in his arms, holdin' him like a real mum."

"Mother – Stop!" Horty cried, making the ringtail dig deeper into my armpit, and then she waved with exaggerated enthusiasm towards the trap and its occupants who were unable to wave back but only hang onto their wooden bench seat through a series of mud-filled ruts; their feet pressed hard against the kickboard.

"Come and have a look at what Alistair's caught." Horty cried even louder, "You too, Neville, you can show it to Sammy – if he doesn't need a change, that is."

"Mother, you must look!"

I studied Lizbeth's brown eyes and for the briefest

moment she changed focus and looked with intent up Plummer Road to feign ignorance of Horty's plaintive cries. At the last second, she tightened the reins and with a lowered voice yelled, 'Whoa Devil!' before pulling the horse and trap up at a point close to the post and rail fence where Horty and I stood.

Through shallow breath as if exhausted from controlling the flighty, yet handsome coal-black colt that Horty's father had given her as a Christmas present, Lizbeth shouted.

"Hello, Alistair. What strange creature have you got there?"

Not wanting to shout in reply and disturb the quite comfortable possum, I asked Horty if she could go over to the trap and ask if the occupants would come to me.

As soon as Horty reached Sniffle's side of the trap, she raised both her hands towards him and indicated by wiggling her fingers that she would take her stepbrother now, even though he looked quite content swaddled in a light blue cotton shawl in Sniffle's chubby arms.

"Thanks for taking care of Sammy, Neville – One would think you'd had a child yourself," Horty said and then looked back at me, pursing her lips so she couldn't laugh.

"Hortense, you were meant to come back with me after mass. I allowed more than enough time for you to walk from St. Augustine's to the Memorial Church." Lizbeth said, glaring at Horty from the whip side of the trap.

"You know how hard it is to hold Samuel on this rough

part of Plummer Road and with a skittish colt like Devil –
Thank goodness, Neville agreed to help."

I watched Horty closely for a reaction as Sniffle handed
Samuel gently down to her. Within seconds she replied
with confidence.

"Sorry Mother, but Principal Miss Ellie Sampson
stopped me as I was walking past Cooblanna House on
my way back to you. She wanted to know if it would be
fine for her to drop by home this afternoon to talk to you
and Father. I said I'm sure they would be happy to receive
you, but I got into a bit of a tizz and felt I needed to get
back home as soon as possible and help Lucia tidy up, so I
accepted a lift with the Wells. By then I had remembered
how you don't like Plummer Road, so I waited for you on
the corner of the beach road. It was only then that I noticed
Alistair halfway up a tree."

Lizbeth appeared to seethe with anger at Horty's broad
explanation, handing Sniffle the reins of the trap without
request and then stepping down carefully onto a level patch
of ground in the centre of the track. With each arm holding up large bundles of white dress she tiptoed over to the
fence.

The first thing I noticed as Lizbeth approached, apart
from how she wore her hair loose like an unpresented girl,
was that her complexion was peaky and only made worse by
circles under her eyes and thin pallid lips.

I was unsure what to make of her appearance and tried

not to believe it had anything to do with Horty's aversion to her.

"What is it, Alistair?" Lizbeth asked without enthusiasm, not looking at the possum, or me, but somewhere in the distance.

"A ringtail possum, Mrs Brown," I replied as brightly as I could considering her disinterest.

"A lotta people call 'em opossums, though. Dunno which name's right."

"Fine," Lizbeth said abruptly and then looked me straight in the eye. "Do you know anything about Miss Ellie Sampson, the principal from the school at Cooblanna? Do you know any of her likes, or dislikes?"

"No, my sister, Millicent, might know more, but I've heard the Sampson sisters run a pretty good school," I replied quite bemused by her question. "The only thing I could say for sure is that the girls like putting on plays. They might want to stage one around your house."

"That may be, Alistair, and I *do know* Millie," Lizbeth responded sharply as if I thought her ignorant of her neighbours or notable Mentone residents. Although, according to Horty, the 'new' Mrs Brown generally kept to herself at church and in the five years since she moved to Mentone from Prahran, rarely ventured outside their home.

"I wish Mr Brown didn't have to go to church in Cheltenham, every week," Lizbeth said quietly as if it was a secret between us.

"Father doesn't *have to* go to church in Cheltenham every week, Mother." Horty cut in with an almost mocking tone as she reached Lizbeth's side, obviously catching her comment.

"The large contractors go to church there and they tell him after mass what materials they're short of – Hasn't he told you?"

"Of course, he has Hortense. I just wish he would take us to church for a change. Even if he would have to go with you to St Augustine's. It would still be nice for both of us."

The possum was now showing signs of restlessness and I could feel a claw scratching me through a hole in my shirt. It was time the quite well-behaved marsupial went back into its hollow, and if possible before it left, distracted Horty and Lizbeth from their rancour; a task which may prove too difficult for man or beast.

"Mrs Brown, I may need Neville's help to put the possum back, if that's fine by you," I said looking to her and then to Sniffle, who nodded his head indicating he was ready to relinquish any more responsibility.

"Why yes. Neville can do as he pleases. I'm sure Hortense and I can get us home from here." Lizbeth replied, and then hesitated before she asked.

"May I touch the possum before we go?"

"Of course, you can, Mrs Brown. Better make it quick, though." I replied eagerly, "I will bring it as close to the rail as I can and careful it might move when you touch it."

I stepped up as high as I could onto the rise before the fence while Lizbeth took off a glove and then tentatively reached her arm over the rail. With fingers shaking mildly, she patted the fur on the possum's back, a huge smile then spread across her face and her brown eyes lit up with glee.

"It is so soft and warm, Alistair. I didn't expect that."

"It's a wonder this one allowed me to grab it from its hole, considering the number of its relatives that've been shot by locals in the last few years."

"I would believe that from the number of shots I hear," Lizbeth said nodding her head as she stepped back from the rail. She then turned to Horty. "Hortense, you don't mind if I ask Alistair and Neville if they would like to come back to La Plage for a quick cup of tea before lunch, seeing they have shown me such kindness."

Horty frowned, appearing to bite her tongue, and I could guarantee not because she didn't want Sniffle and I to come back to her house, as we had visited there many times before, but perhaps wondering what was behind Lizbeth's generosity. I had a thought.

*Lizbeth may want Sniffle and I to tend to Devil while she and Horty prepare for their visitor, and later to show Miss Sampson around the property if Mr Brown hasn't arrived back from church.*

—•—

# CHAPTER TWO

# The Principal

ॐ

"**Lucky it was me** and not Perce Hudd who helped out Mrs Brown." Sniffle stated through heavy breath as we hoofed our way on loose sand up the last hundred yards of Plummer Road before we were to reach the drive of Horty's family home, La Plage. A house that for the last two years had sat resplendent in white on a rise facing south-east towards the beach.

"He would a' shot the possum outta yuh hands and kept a good hold of Samuel at the same time."

As if foretold, a shot rang out to the right of us from the vacant Naples Estate, a shortcut we sometimes took to get to the shops in Mentone.

"That's probably Perce now, and I wouldn't doubt he'd've had a go at the possum – He's a bloody danger with a rifle," I replied, nodding to Sniffle, whose face had turned a deeper tone of crimson the further we walked up the hill. The coolness of the previous few days following a thunderstorm only a short reprieve from the hot spell that had continued relentlessly since a week before Christmas.

Sniffle lifted his peaked cap and then wiped his forehead free of perspiration, before loosening the high and stiff collar of his sweat-stained shirt.

"Yuh know, you and Perce are the luckiest buggers gettin' around. Yuh never have to go to stupid church." Sniffle declared while drawing in large gulps of air, and then breathing them out just as hard. "I'd give away all my good agates for that!"

Sniffle stopped and then turned his rotund frame towards me. "Hang on for a sec will yuh?" and then took in more large breaths before he asked, "Perce's family have never gone to church, but how'd *you* get out of it?"

"Keep goin' Sniff and I'll tell yuh…"

I found it hard to believe that I had missed an entire year of church, and he was the first person to ask or dare ask me why. I assumed most adults knew the reason and avoided the subject. Sniffle reluctantly took off again and I was just as reluctant to tell him the truth.

"My dad says the gardens need lookin' after seven days a week now, 'specially since the hot weather's come in. He's been drawin' water from the Glebe Spring every other day up until the change … and Mum has so many orders for her candles and honey."

Sniffle looked at me sideways as if doubtful of my explanation, which he should have been because what I had heard while lying in bed and through paper-thin walls was not what he, the congregation of our church or most locals would like to hear. Dad had lent for one day, his dray and himself, to move timber for the construction of a new church not a huge distance from his own, and word had got back to him that a member of his congregation had said, 'for a person who leaves little on the plate, it's rich that he should help a church gilded in wealth.'

Dad was ropeable to say the least and refused to attend church until the responsible party came forward and offered an apology. As I knew the perpetrator, it was unlikely he had the fortitude to front my dad. From a genial man, Dad then withdrew from social life, leaving behind an angry man who barely resembled my father. He said he would leave it up to the rest of the family if we wished to leave the congregation.

Mum suggested to Millie and I that we should stay home on Sundays and keep Dad company, especially as soon after this incident, my older brother Reg suddenly decided to leave home.

⋙

A short distance from the drive at La Plage, Sniffle asked. "D'yuh reckon that's the Sampson lady, Horty was goin' on about, just turnin' the bend?" He then pointed up Plummer Road. "...or one of her sisters?"

I strained my eyes to see at the corner of Florence Street a horse and buggy sway, straighten and then drive towards us at a good rate. The figure in blue holding the reins appeared to be a young lady and as she had already passed the only other residence down this quiet lane, and the Browns were not expecting anyone else.

"It's got to be her, Sniff. We'd better put the Browns in the know." I grabbed Sniffle by the arm to make him move faster than his usual shuffle.

The drive at La Plage forked midway along its length; one lane to the right in the direction of the stables, the other directly to the front entrance where it then curved around a lily pond to reconnect as an exit. To me, this was the most magnificent out of a dozen grand homes in Mentone, and although consisting of only one storey had extensive iron lacework and a large bay window; a house which at times gave me a twinge of envy as it was so much bigger and grander than my ramshackle home.

My boots made thuds on the boards of the veranda before I knocked rapidly on the lead lighting of the front door. A concerned face soon appeared through the glass panelling and a second later the door opened with the Browns' housekeeper, Lucia, filling the space.

"You know you boys can't come in this way," Lucia stated

abruptly in her indistinct foreign accent, "Go around to the back porch where you normally go." She then pointed sternly to her left.

Lucia was squat with plastered flat brown hair; a tight bun at the rear, white maid's cap at the front, she was also humourless when it came to engaging with Sniffle or me. Horty often referred to her as Lucifer.

"Can yuh let the Browns know that we saw Miss Ellie Sampson from the Cooblanna school driving in a rush to get here? She's only a minute down the road!" I exclaimed without taking a breath before she was able to shut the door.

"I haven't heard of such a thing," Lucia said as a put-off while maintaining a hint of uncertainty in her eyes.

"Hortense spoke to her after church – She *is* coming!" Sniffle said jumping in before I could say the same.

"Alright then, go!" Lucia said abruptly and then slammed the door on us. Her footsteps could then be heard stomping down the hall towards the kitchen at the far end of the house.

"Where is everyone, Sniff?" I asked, to which he just shrugged his shoulders and began to walk towards the stables. Not long after I had caught up to him we both stopped abruptly in our tracks after passing the last brush panel before the stalls, surprised to see Lizbeth with her back pressed against a stable door and Mr Brown kissing her passionately; Horty or Samuel, nowhere in sight.

Sniffle and I tried to backtrack behind the brush panel

to avoid any embarrassment, but my boots and Sniffle's shoes made scraping sounds on the gravel that could not be ignored. Mr Brown stepped back from Lizbeth and put up his hand for us to stop.

"Hello, gentlemen." He said with the intimation of a slur in his voice, his cheeks a shiny red. "Why leave when you just got here?"

Sniffle and I froze on the spot as Mr Brown stretched out an arm and pointed towards Lizbeth.

"Isn't my wife beautiful, Alistair? – What sayeth you, Neville?"

I was unsure what this display was about, but Lizbeth seemed at ease; and although covering her face with both hands, allowed a giggle to slip out.

"She is very pretty." Sniffle replied, engaging too closely with Mr Brown's sentiment for my liking. Before I had to agree, Horty burst through the kitchen's flyscreen door.

"Hello, for one's information, Principal Miss Ellie Sampson from Cooblanna has arrived and has Lucia in attendance." Horty pronounced as if a bib and tuck butler, and then turned to Sniffle and me. "Alistair and Neville, do you mind helping Lucia tend to the principal's horse, freeing her up to visit our home. I shall provide tea and scones for you, forthwith."

Horty smiled at us and then lifted her chin at her dad and Lizbeth before turning on the spot and returning through the screen door.

Sniffle and I found a wide-eyed Lucia on the far side of the lily pond, holding the reins of the principal's horse while trying to stop it raising and lowering its head in agitation; Miss Sampson stood nearby in a navy skirt and light blue blouse shushing gently into the horse's turned back ear.

To my surprise as Sniffle and I approached from behind the buggy, Miss Sampson began speaking to Lucia in a foreign language, which was almost certainly German.

"Versuchen sie, die schnauze des pferdes zu tätscheln."

Sniffle opened his mouth wide enough to let in a multitude of flies, while Lucia nodded her head and began rubbing the muzzle of the principal's horse with her free hand. Within seconds the horse lowered its head and calmed for the present.

"Vielen dank. Erstaunliches ergebnis." Lucia replied to whatever Miss Sampson had said.

Lizbeth and Mr Brown then appeared on the porch and immediately gave little waves to the principal.

"Thank you, Lucia, Alistair, and Neville, for putting yourself out to look after Roebuck. I must apologize for his behaviour as he is normally such a calm horse – It may be the north wind." A warm smile then appeared on Miss Sampson's cherubic face.

"Neville, Principal Meagher informs me that you were

dux of your class last year, and Alistair, you were not far behind. I am sure you will both do well in the Merit."

Sniffle and I replied that we would try our best. As Miss Sampson walked up the steps and onto the veranda to be received by the Browns, I wondered how at such a youthful age she had been able to achieve a prestigious position and acquire so much knowledge. Also, what nature does she possess that would make her interested in the academic level of two boys, inconsequential to her, who live on the fringes of a small village and would never be attending her girls' school? Likely, a good one.

In the meantime, Sniffle had taken the reins from Lucia, leaving her to grumble to herself as she stormed off to the back of the house.

"How can the Browns expect me to be a good housekeeper and a horse minder at the same time?"

Sniffle and I took the horse and buggy around to the stables, watered and then brushed down the principal's dapple-grey colt; an animal that turned out to be quite easy to manage. Time then began to drag for Sniffle and me, eventually ending up with us mooching around the water trough kicking up dirt. So, we then decided to brush down Mr Brown's own temperamental horse, Chester, and eventually even grooming Devil, to fill in more time.

Sniffle and I both knew we would be in trouble for being late for lunch at home when Horty poked her head out of the screen door and waved for us to come over.

"Come here – Quick!" Horty whispered, "I got some news for yuh."

I was running out of interest for what drama Miss Sampson's visit was causing inside. I was hungry, smelt of horse and possum, and ready to go home. Horty handed us a tray through the door with a pot of tea, a small jug of milk, two China cups with spoons, and two scones with jam and cream on top, to some relief. Speaking at breakneck speed she said that the principal was a lovely lady and wanted to know if the Browns could take in a late enrolment as a boarder, a girl from a farm near Wodonga, who had already gained some renown as a stage performer.

"Bad news is Miss Sampson offered a half scholarship for me to go to Cooblanna," Horty then sighed. "This day's goin' down the Brasco."

Horty closed the kitchen door and then pressed her lips and nose against the screen and said pigheadedly through it.

"Just lettin' yuh know – I ain't goin' to Cooblanna!" Horty then banged the door with both hands as she left.

Sniffle and I scoffed down our tea and scones, both in a race to get ourselves out of here and back home as quickly as possible. As soon as we had taken our last swallow of tea we opened the screen door, placed the tray and its contents on the kitchen bench and then both shouted in harmony into the quiet house, 'Thanks for the tea and scones', before letting the screen door slam behind us and running for home.

—•—

"Alistair, come out the back, *now* please." Called my dad from near the woodshed, his voice penetrating deep inside the house as far as my room.

A shiver of dread ran through me on hearing these words, as all my recent talks with Dad had ended up with me getting a lecture on subjects of which I knew little, and any attempt to reason was pointless, as it only made him more irrational. Mum, Millie, and I, had no choice but to walk on eggshells every day.

—•—

"Where've you been? You're too late for lunch by a long shot, and don't bother interrupting yuh mum – She's busy makin' candles." Dad declared as soon as I poked my head around the corner of the shed and saw him standing in the dark staring down the length of the tea-tree hedge that formed the boundary of our property.

"Mrs Brown asked Neville and me back to her place for a cup of tea," I replied firmly trying not to show fear. "Neville helped her drive the trap up Plummer Road."

"Didn't have to spoil you, too," Dad grumbled and then turned to face me.

"I spoke to Principal Meagher today after he got back from church, an' told him I wanted you to leave school at midday tomorrow, so you can go and see Mr Rennie at his bakery."

Dad picked up pieces of split wood and placed them on top of a stack resting against the corrugated iron wall of the shed. I stood in silence wondering what Mr Rennie had to do with me.

"Your principal argued that the first day back was important, but I told him a job that could put money in the palm of your hand for the rest of your life was more important."

Still baffled by his statements, I took two steps back into the sunlight.

"Did Mr Rennie ask for me?"

"No need for Jock to ask for anyone," My dad responded sharply, "I want you to go and see him while he's still got a vacancy in his shop."

"But I'm not a baker," I replied quietly, trying not to antagonize my father.

"Don't be smart, Alistair. There's a vacancy of some kind because your brother caused it and it's up to this family to rectify his loss – People talk about us enough."

"You're thirteen now. I left school well before then."

I wanted to argue, but knew it wasn't worth it. I had no

real interest in school, but I also knew I wasn't ready to leave it. At least I was smart enough to understand that.

# Jock's Bakery

**LATE JANUARY 1905**

**I FOUND MR RENNIE** in the backyard of his bakery, situated just off a small lane that ran south from Florence Street and at the back of the tearooms that sold his bread and pastries in Mentone Parade. He was poking with a stick a small fire in a pot belly stove while feeding it ripped paper and patches of flour bags. The fire smoked and then flared as he moved the material from one side of the pot to the other to allow more air to reach the flame. He didn't seem to notice me watching him as I shook with trepidation at the prospect, of how, in the proceeding minutes, my life was about to change forever.

I knew he was Scottish, everyone called him Jock, but with splayed feet, a short rotund body swimming in a sagging suit, and his head topped with a tattered green hat, he could have been a real-life leprechaun, perched over his smoking pot of gold. I could have laughed but forced myself to remember that I was here to sacrifice my life to ease the conscience of my father. All because of the way my brother had left the service of Mr Rennie. Reg just didn't show up for work one day.

"I noo yuh there." Mr Rennie said in his thick brogue, continuing to poke the fire while facing away from me. "You'll no get a game of tiggy in my home toon."

"Sorry, I should have made myself known," I replied sheepishly. "I'm Alistair. Alistair Lundy. My dad told me to come and see you."

"Did he noo? – And I do noo who you are, laddie," Mr Rennie said and then threw the stick into the smouldering fire and faced me. "Reg happened to give me and the lads a tip aboot you over lunch one day."

"He said it were you who cut the head off the pesky snake at the Dowling's hoos, not the missus."

"Did he?" I replied, taken aback that my brother who rarely spoke to me at the best of times and was the only one I had mentioned the snake incident to, would tell, or even brag about me lopping the head off the poor tiger snake that had wandered over the Dowling's back porch in search of a stray mouse to eat.

"He did and he also said you liked a cup of tea and scones." Mr Rennie said and then chuckled to himself. "Lucky, I oon a bakery, hey laddie? Come inside, the kettle's always on the boil."

My first impression of Mr Rennie as I followed him

around the side of the high building and in through a screened door into what appeared to be a lunchroom, was that as a boss he might be easy going enough, and had a particular sense of humour, but I was told by my brother that he got more than his pound of flesh from each worker and was also subject to sullen moods when things didn't go his way.

"Do you know why Mrs Dowling said she killed the snake?" Mr Rennie asked as he picked up a ceramic teapot from a table that stretch the length of the room. I was not surprised he was curious about the snake incident as it was news for a week in a small village like Mentone, which was a sleepy hollow for a large part of the year.

"No, I just happened to be walking past their place, when I heard Mrs Dowling scream. When I got around the back, she'd already hit the snake with a mattock. I just finished it off ... She was in a flap. I'm not surprised she didn't remember I was there."

Mr Rennie washed tea leaves out from the pot into a trough and then pointed for me to grab two cups from wooden dowels mounted on the wall nearest the proofing room door. One dowel had a cup with Jock written above it in chalk, the other, Reg; below that dowel on a hook was a high white hat sitting on top of an apron still covered in flour.

"I'm guessing your dad has it in his mind that it's good

business for me to exchange a boy for Reg, an almost groon man, who could put out dozens of bonnie loaves a day?"

"I can learn to bake," I replied as confidently as I could after seeing Mr Rennie's mood harden. "And do deliveries from tomorrow."

"How old are you, laddie?"

"Turned thirteen a few months back."

"Now, I'm askin' you straight oot. Do you want to be a baker?" Mr Rennie said deliberately, placing more than enough scoops of tea in the pot without taking his eyes off me. After a time, I replied clearly.

"No."

Followed by a sigh, Mr Rennie said quietly. "Sit doon, Alistair."

Mr Rennie rubbed his stubbled chin for a time and then continued.

"Yuh noo, nair you probably don't noo. Workin', 'specially bakin', is no just aboot makin' great bread. It's aboot doin' your job, day in day oot, with a smile on your face."

Mr Rennie brought the boiled kettle from the stove and then filled the large pot to half full before stirring its contents with a dessert spoon.

"I need lads with stories to tell. I need a roar of laughter when a fart slips oot ... Silence is a killer at work. Your brother was quiet."

I lowered my head, knowing he was right.

Reg was happy on his own and would have hated the

heat and closeness in here. He loved riding, even on the coldest days and never let up on how sleeping under the stars, like a drover, must be the life – He should never have let himself become a baker.

"I was the happiest man; the day Reg didn't show up for work." Mr Rennie said plainly.

Mr Rennie poured two cups of tea and warned that if I ever did deliveries as a carter, against accepting offers for a cup of tea on the way, as, apart from regularly needing to stop for a pee, the milk in most homes was often on the turn.

"Anyhoo, enough with work. I heard that you and your mate, Neville, and the Brown girl, were trying to trap animals over the school holidays. Is that troo?" Mr Rennie asked appearing more relaxed now that we had cleared the air over Reg's leaving.

"Me, Neville, and Horty – Hortense," I began enthusiastically, "Had an idea to trap a native cat and take it to anywhere having a carnival day and charge people to look at it. There's not too many of 'em left now. Lots of 'em were shot near our place."

"Did you trap one?"

"No, didn't even see one."

"Yuh noo, I had an idea a wee bit like that when I was your age." Said Mr Rennie as he sat forward cradling his cup, engaged with the subject. "I fancied myself as a sprint-er when I was a laddie and thought I was fast enough to catch a wild cat in the brae. One afternoon, I spied a cat in the heather, and it was away. I ran after it at full tilt, all the way up the side of a hill until I was out of puff. All it did was look back at me as if to say, 'Well, laddie, you're a duffer – You're in my realm noo!' ... Just as well, 'cause if I'd caught up to it, it would a' ripped my shimmy to shreds."

I had a sip of tea and looked across at Mr Rennie with his crumpled suit and greying hair and found it hard to imagine him as a young lad running wildly through the highlands after a native cat; a cat which on all accounts was much larger and nastier than our version. Mr Rennie took two scones out from under a fly guard, put them on a plate and then offered both to me. He continued.

"After that, I gave up on trying to catch a wild cat and concentrated more on endurance and not just speed – just like the cat had. One day while I was running in the foot-hills behind my hoos in Elgin, I caught a glimpse of a beas-tie out of the corner of my eye. I stopped to look but it was gone. The next day I went back to the same hill and kept my wits aboot me. Sure enough, a wild cat, not as muckle as the other, was shadowing me through heather and burn."

"Was it hunting you?" I asked, now engrossed in his story.

"That's what I first thought, Alistair. So, I took care it didn't get behind me. But noo, I was wrong. I changed course and it changed to suit. I went faster, it went faster. I slowed down, it slowed down – The bairn was just wanting someone to play with."

Mr Rennie put his cup down and looked me in the eye. "I would never put such a spirited beastie in a cage."

There was a silence between us, because I knew what Mr Rennie was saying, and it stung. It hurt because I would be no better, in fact, worse than Perce Hudd, who paid no mind in shooting an unsuspecting animal out of a tree. In a cage, its death couldn't come quick enough.

Mr Rennie topped up his cup and then put a dribble in mine.

"This is what I'm gonna do," Mr Rennie stated with intent. "An' there'll be no discussion aboot it from your dad – or you."

I braced myself for what my future might hold.

"I'll put you on a twelve-month trial. You'll stay at school and work every Saturday doin' deliveries or scrapin' bits of dough off the floor 'round here. And you'll no slow doon my delivery manny, or you'll cop it from him and me."

My mind was in a whirl as I tried to quickly comprehend what this would entail. It didn't take me long to realize that his demands were more than reasonable. Mr Rennie then said less earnestly.

"We'll have a good look at each other and noo soon enough if you're for here."

I took a sip of my tea and then studied the leaves swirling around the bottom of the cup. By being fair, Mr Rennie had also given my father no room to argue for something more permanent now. I could only make one decision.

"I'll give it my best, Mr Rennie," I promised genuinely and then remembered that Sniffle, Horty, and I wanted to go trapping again. "...but can I ask if you need me next Sat..."

Mr Rennie jumped in before I could say more, aware that this occasion had come at short notice for both of us.

"The one after will do fine, Alistair."

# CHAPTER FOUR

# ...Often Go Awry!

**HORTY AND SNIFFLE TOLD** me to wait for them under the awnings outside of Harkin's produce store in Mentone Parade after I had finished talking to Mr Rennie. They had pestered me all morning at school about what to say and how to stand up for myself if things weren't going well, and said they desperately wanted to know the result of their dubious advice.

In the end, the outcome was far better than I could have ever imagined; being able to work and continue school for at least one more year was not in my thoughts. The long walk to Cheltenham to go to school would no longer be a drudge for me, as it was for most of the local kids who cursed the day Mentone Public School was closed.

While I was waiting, I filled in time by saying hello to customers as they went into the cash store, most of whom I knew by name, and then held the door open for them later when they came out with their arms loaded with goods. In the grain store to the right of the main entrance, Ernie, the storeman, and one of Perce Hudd's brothers, of which there were many, was toiling away manfully.

He was weighing sorghum, sowing ears on bags of pollard, and stooking hay to the rear; his back often bent, his hair and frayed leather apron covered in flecks of chaff.

"How are yuh, Loon?" Ernie asked with a strain in his deep voice as he dragged a particularly large bag of potatoes towards a dray waiting on the street.

"Lookin' for Reg are yuh?" He added through a cheeky grin. I didn't need that comment after Mr Rennie had put any bad feelings about Reg's leaving to rest.

"Hi, Ernie," I replied cheerfully, not wanting to let on how little I thought of his remark. "You're workin' like a threshing machine in there."

"Have to," Ernie said, stopping to lean the bag against himself while noticing my continued annoyance. "Sorry Loon. That was a low blow." A few seconds later the penny dropped, and he added,

"Yuh dinkum don't know where Reg is, do yuh?"

I didn't want to say anything but came up with, "Nuh, nobody's told me anythin', Ernie ... suppose he's drovin' somewhere."

"Give me a hand to lift this bag of spuds onto the dray an' I'll tell yuh where he is." Ernie declared already leaning the bag back, so I had to take the bottom. I grabbed it by the ears and waited for his signal.

"On three ... one, two, three." He called at the same time

as I realized how much better he had of this lift. We hauled the bag onto the side of the dray with a grunt and then pushed it over the back wheels. Ernie took off his gloves and leant against the metal frame.

"He's camped the other side of Carrum Swamp, mainly draggin' cattle and various carrion out of it for one of Balcombe's mobs. An' accordin' to my brother Max, who spied him in Mordialloc – he's as happy as a pig in shit."

"Good to hear that, Ernie" I replied nodding my head as if satisfied by this news. However, in truth, extremely disappointed for not being told any of this by either of my parents, who must know. Or, by Reg himself, in a letter or by searching me out one day. Reg could have handled leaving home so much better.

"What are yuh doin' hangin' around here, anyway?" Ernie asked curiously while pulling his gloves back on. I hesitated before answering.

"I went to see Mr Rennie about a job." I said truthfully and before he could pry any further into my or my family's business, I added, "Gotta go now Ernie, gotta find Horty and Sniffle.

◆•◆

After leaving Ernie in Mentone Parade, I turned into Florence Street only to see another Hudd coming towards me.

*Is there no end to their number?*

Perce, tall and lean, was walking beside short and chubby Sniffle, both managing to push each other in the shoulder in the way great mates do, which in truth they hadn't been before I left school at lunchtime, but who knows what a new school year could bring. Horty was following behind them, talking to, of all people, a nun, who like a black and white swan was leading a brood of eight female students back to the new and burgeoning Brigidine Boarding School for Young Ladies at the old Como House.

No sooner had Perce and Sniffle walked into the sun after leaving the canopy of the Florence Street Tobacconist, one of the half dozen shops locally that sold the chopped leaf, than they bailed me up near a streetlamp so that Horty could let the nun and her clutch pass by.

"Bye for now," Horty called as she waved to the nun, and then said while screwing up her face, "I ain't goin' there, either. They're gonna have more girls than Cooblanna. Be just the same though, girls cryin' on each other's shoulders one day, stabbin' each other in the back, the next." Horty then shook her head.

"How many girls' schools does this village need?"

No sooner had Horty finished decrying all things wrong with girls' schools, in a poor attempt to stave off her inevitable entry into one of their folds, than Perce pushed in front of her, and give me a light punch on the shoulder.

"Still goin' trappin' on Saturday, Loon?" Perce asked, and

then turned back to look at Sniffle as if they had already worked out a plan. "I've heard of a good spot where a few native cats have been seen."

I looked over at Sniffle who was conveniently studying the tobacconist's window.

"Sounds great, Perce, but I gotta problem," I replied, then thought I'd see if any of my good mates remembered why I had left school early.

"Whadayuh on about, Loon?" Sniffle asked, returning to squint his beady eyes at me.

"I know," Horty cut in and then deliberately stepped in front of Perce. "How'd yuh go with old Jock?"

"Good Hort. He only wants me to work on Saturdays. Trouble is – he's dead set against shootin' or trappin' animals, 'specially native cats ... Somethin' happened to him when he was in Scotland."

Perce turned around and kicked stones into the gutter, going silent as a young lad who loved shooting things would.

"Jock says fishin's the real sport," I added even though Mr Rennie hadn't mentioned it.

Perce while still turned away and studying his feet, quietly said.

"My dad did bring me back a new fishin' rod at Christmas and I ain't used it yet."

"I ain't been fishin' for yonks either, Perce." Sniffle said as he went over and stood beside his new best friend.

"Where's the place where yuh saw native cats, Perce?"

Horty asked, and then while Perce and Sniffle's backs were still turned, opened her eyes as wide as she could, indicating she had a plan of her own.

"Out the back of the Keys' farm in Beaumaris," Perce replied as he returned to face Horty and me, his bottom lip still down. "Some pretty thick bush out that way. Thought yuh'd know that."

"I ain't never been past the Keys' place before," Horty said screwing up her face towards Perce and then quickly added, "We could go out that way an' see if there's any native cats around and then go down to Ricketts Point to do some fishin'.'"

Horty then took up the pose of a fashionable lady looking around the scene and added in an equally posh voice, "...and I've heard lately there's been loads of toffs piling off trams there. We could go and see them wandering around the beach looking each other up and down."

"People 'round here ought a' call *you* a toff, Horty," Perce stated without any attempt at humour and then said while rocking his head confidently from side to side.

"Livin' in a fine house with yuh own maid."

Perce was gormless at the best of times, but this time he had shoved his oar in the wrong pond. Horty's back went straight up.

"You, Percival Hudd, know I grew up in a house half the size of yours," She responded sharply, showing him her pointer, and glaring into his eyes. "... and I know the copper lady who comes in every week to wash your skiddy drawers – and yours are the worst!"

Horty then turned her hand into a fist.

"...so, anyone 'round here calls me a toff will get a punch in the head!"

Perce was a good foot taller than Horty and stronger as a boy, but what advantage he held in strength and stature was more than matched by his opponent's spirit. They commenced to stare each other down.

The silence that ensued as Perce and Horty tried to win the mental battle soon became annoying for me, and certainly for an easily distracted Sniffle. We desperately needed to break the stalemate.

"Hey, I just remembered, Jock gave me some new pastries to try," I declared loudly and cheerfully, "He says the bakers make a special treat for 'emselves from leftover dough an' no customers ever gets to try 'em."

Sniffle, who was always hungry, was the first to forget about the deadlock. Perce looked over at me and then back at Horty with more concentration. Horty's stance never wavered. I then pulled out from deep inside my pocket a small brown packet and began to unwrap each fold, only to find a pile of broken pastries.

"Bloody hell!" I exclaimed in annoyance, realizing I had crushed the pastry while I was helping Ernie load the potatoes. Perce and Horty gave themselves a brief reprieve from their concentration to peek sideways to see what had caused my outburst. Meanwhile, Sniffle studied closely the crumbs and scattered pieces of pastry, and then said to our dismay.

"If yuh eat all the tiny bits. T'is just the same as eatin' a whole."

Horty and Perce burst out laughing at the same time, almost spitting over each other's faces. I joined them, while Sniffle looked dumbfounded at us, oblivious to his gaffe.

After the relief of ending the stand-off, we all decided to give Horty's plan a go.

"Ricketts Point it is, then." I said and then we all shook hands on it.

"An' we could even go for a swim if it gets too hot." I added to a nod from Sniffle and Perce.

Horty immediately rolled her eyes and said sarcastically.

"Sooner see a native cat's bum."

⬤•⬤

On our way home, Perce, Sniffle, Horty, and I walked with our arms over each other's shoulders, excited and talking non-stop about what we would need to bring on what would not only be our best fishing trip, but a great adventure, things like; rods and worms, sandwiches and biscuits and plenty of water as the weather was likely to be staying hot.

Perce was the first to leave us at Milan Street and shortly

afterwards Sniffle at Plummer Road. It wasn't until after I had waved and said 'see yuh t'morra' to Horty at the bottom of the drive at La Plage and began to walk to my home which was the next property than I realized that Horty and I had walked with our arms over each other's shoulders for the entire trip from Florence Street.

❧

# CHAPTER FIVE

# Mother's Milk

As I climbed over the top rail of the home paddock fence, I noticed Millie leaving Mum's honey shed and heading past the stable back to our house. I thought about letting her go in peace but then decided, no, I had good news to share.

"Millie – Stop will yuh!" She immediately spun around to face me, startled by how loudly I had called.

"Whadayuh callin' like that for, Loon?" Millie returned and then began an easy and relaxed walk towards me with the low sun casting shadows in the paddock behind. A smile then formed as Millie remembered where Dad had told me to go to after school.

"How'd you go at the bakery?"

"Great, Mill!" I replied cheerfully. "I got a job, but I'm still goin' to school."

"How does *that* work?" Millie asked in her usual nonchalant manner.

"It works that I work for Jock on Saturdays." I declared,

jumping off the fence and inside for joy with the luck I had had today. "Not sure how Dad will take it, but no-one can change Jock's mind, be sure on that."

"I wouldn't get too cocky if I were you. You know how determined he can get."

Millie's seriousness soon gave way as she added.

"Anyway, Loon, well done. Before I forget, can you tell Horty I'll be starting later at Taylors for the rest of the week, so I can walk to school with her if she likes. I'll let her know what I've heard about Cooblanna. Might sway her one way or the other."

Millie then took off in a slow walk back towards the house, saying as she left,

"By the way, Mum wants to see yuh. I'm goin' inside to get tea started."

⊷•⊷

I peered through the tight opening to the honey shed, past batten doors held back by stacked beehives on one side and long discarded straw skeps on the other; a single candle filled the warm interior with a golden glow. I then breathed in the amazing, sweet nectar that permeated every corner of Mum's small, yet cosy workspace. Along her wooden work bench, glass jars, small pots and pans, and a shallow tray had been crammed; a wisp of smoke escaped from the pot belly stove at the end of the shed.

At that moment, Mum was leaning over the only clear space on the bench, her fingers curling the bottom edge of a thin beeswax sheet.

"Come over here, Alistair. I can't stop while the wax is plying." She said in her soft, never angry voice.

I stood quietly out of her way and watched in amazement as she formed wax over a wick that extended beyond both ends of the sheet. With speed and dexterity, she rolled the wax into a tight cylinder, only once having to unravel a small section to straighten. Once satisfied, she smoothed the join and then cut off one end of the wick, finally trimming the other to finger width.

"There, that will do for the day," Mum said while placing the candle into a box with others and then giving me a warm smile. "I heard you outside. You got a job at Jock's bakery."

"I did and for only one day a week, for this year," I stated after returning her smile.

"Old Jock's let me off the hook – for sure."

"Don't ever let your dad hear you say that." Came as a repeat of Millie's warning and as stern as Mum had ever mustered.

Mum then moved a dust-covered beehive off a low wooden chest; another layer of dust became unsettled as she opened the chest's lid. Inside were half a dozen jars covered with cloth and tied with string below the lid. Mum pulled one jar out.

"When Reginald received the news that he would be doing his time as a baker with Mr Rennie, he was so excited. You would have been too young to notice ... It didn't turn out for the best, it seems."

I held my tongue. Mum didn't need to know that Jock was pleased Reg had gone.

"That evening Reginald came out to the shed as well, and I thought as he was taking his first step into becoming his own man, he could partake in what used to be your dad's only vice, a tipple I make from time to time, and one which your dad said was 'mother's milk' after each first sip."

Mum undid the string and unwrapped the cloth surrounding the glass jar, revealing a honey-coloured liquid inside. She unscrewed the lid with resistance and then placed the jar's opening under my nose. A honey smell was there, but also a combination of every wildflower in our vicinity melted into one; banksia, tea-tree, gum, and wattle stood out, as did a multitude of other scents including the crisp contrast of apple, surely added by bees working our orchards.

"Do you like the smell?" Mum asked while confident I would.

"It's incredible. Just smells of everything around here in spring."

"It should," Mum replied, then placed the open jar on the bench and searched under a clean cloth, soon producing two small jars.

"Would you like to try a sip?" I nodded my head

immediately and Mum poured a small quantity of the liquid into each jar and handed me the smallest of the pours.

"Take a tiny sip first, Alistair," Mum said and then raised her jar in front of me. "So, here's to you, for getting your first job."

I took the smallest of sips and felt a tingle on my tongue. The viscous liquid then warmed the back of my throat as it slid down into my stomach, from where it radiated heat throughout my body. There was still a taste of honey, but a large part of the sweetness had been replaced by an unnatural flavour that took my breath away. I suddenly felt lightheaded, my cheeks began to glow, and I couldn't help myself coughing at the floor away from Mum.

"Are you right, Alistair?" Mum asked, placing a huge grin on her face as she patted my back. "Don't worry, it's a normal reaction when you first try liquor mead – Reginald had to go outside and be sick."

"No wonder Dad stopped drinking it," I said without thinking. Mum's face lost its grin as she turned to gaze out the shed door.

"He will again one day, mark my words."

I had said the wrong thing, but that wouldn't stop me from saying more, as Millie and I had had enough of constantly being on edge in our own home. It was no life for us to have to avoid our father's company. I'm sure Mum was copping it worse and must wonder what became of the gentle man she said she married.

"Mum, what happened to Dad?" I asked straight out, no longer caring that it may be the wrong thing to say. "And why isn't Horty's dad his friend anymore?" There was an extended silence, and I was about to say sorry when Mum spoke.

"Avenal and your dad aren't enemies. Be clear on that. It would be easy to blame May and her sickness – No, sorry I said that." Mum said turning back to look at me, her eyes beginning to well with tears. "I know this is hard on you and Millie, but please give your father more time."

"Avenal and May were our closest friends for so long. We bought our blocks on the same day, and we were the only market gardeners near the slopes when we moved in. We had to build everything from scratch and out of thick scrub. You can't believe how lonely it was at times, but the four of us kept each other going. We laughed and joked by making up silly pranks and telling outrageous stories about how rich we would be one day. But it was sheer stubbornness that stopped us from failing."

Mum had a sip from her jar and then took mine and placed it on the bench.

"Hortense was only young when May started saying things that were a nonsense. She came good for a while, so we thought it may have come about from exhaustion after a bout of pleurisy. One day she abused two ladies in the Emporium, with no justification according to the Harkins. That night after tea, Avenal said her words became slurred and she could no longer stand on her own."

Mum took in deep breaths and a sadness spread across her face, which she fought hard not to show.

"No doctors called around this way at the time, so we had to take her to one in Brighton, one that we were told was good. It took all our combined monies just so he would see her. He said that an infection had established itself in her brain that could go by itself or become worse. He recommended that May be placed in the asylum in Charman Road, where he would give her quinine on his monthly rounds, a drug which he said had shown some promise. Avenal wouldn't have a bar of May being placed in the asylum, saying that no-one who went in, ever came out. He stormed out of the clinic with May and said he would find a way to care for her at home."

"Fortunately, the district nurse who lived in Cheltenham had heard of May's condition and arrived the next night, saying she would call every couple of days and lessen any symptoms. In between Millie and I helped to bathe and feed her. We kept you and Horty away as best we could, you didn't need to see how sick she became. Avenal was so embarrassed that he couldn't even pay the nurse the smallest compensation for her time, which she wouldn't have taken anyway. In the end, he became obsessed with making money to provide May with better care. For good or bad, the rights to lay out the local water reticulation came up and nobody wanted it. The locals had learned to live fine on tanks. Little did they know a run of droughts was coming."

"Avenal then threw himself into getting a crew together to dig miles of trenches. All of it on the never-never. The men he got were the dregs; rough, hard-drinking men who no-one else would touch. It was at the time when contractors were laying out estates around Mentone, and soon after a host of land grabbers financed him. By that time, Avenal and your dad had begun to move in different circles."

"Only six months later, with no major complications. May passed away in her sleep."

Mum steadied her breathing before adding.

"You see, the criticism that came from our church wasn't the reason your dad changed. Having little or no money was one of them, but what really hurt him was losing the friendship we had with Avenal and May."

Mum took me into her arms and said softly. "I'm so glad you've remained friends with Hortense."

❖

## CHAPTER SIX

# *Red Desert*

## EARLY FEBRUARY 1905

ACCORDING TO HORTY, HER step-mother Lizbeth, had turned into the 'biggest blowfly in the ointment' of her life, and had on Thursday, only two days out from what we were sure would be our finest fishing trip, threatened to prevent Horty from going with Perce, Sniffle, and I to Ricketts Point.

'I'd prefer that you participate less in rough and tumble boys' activities,' Lizbeth had apparently said, 'and spend more time in the company of your own gender'. With Horty's recent black mark for not meeting her 'new mum' after church last Sunday, and with Lizbeth's general opinion that 'Hortense' was failing to display sufficient 'young ladylike qualities', she insisted that Horty accompany her to a small tea party organized by Principal Sampson at Cooblanna House on Saturday afternoon, for a group of local mothers and their daughters, put on, I suspect, in the hope of filling the last few student vacancies.

Again, according to Horty, she put on quite an esteemed performance in front of her father and his new wife that 'the whole world should a' seen', saying that to deny her friends of her company during such an important and much anticipated event, 'would be a travesty of justice of the poorest form'. Her father agreed. Lizbeth was not happy.

*Horty Brown is no good, chop her up for firewood*
*If she is no good for that, give her to the old tom cat*

Was sung melodically and stridently by a young lady who sat alone on a long yellow wooden bench on top of a horse-drawn tram as it clip-clopped up beside Horty, Sniffle, Perce, and me on Balcombe Road, less than half an hour after we had set off in the cool of Saturday morning to begin our round-about trip through Beaumaris to Ricketts Point to do some fishing and take in the sights; still marching side by side and still bursting with excitement for what may lay ahead on what we hoped would stay a perfectly sunny day.

The tram then slowed as it approached the turn off into Tramway Parade. Straw boaters, brightly decorated wide-brimmed chapeaux and an assortment of bowlers and fedoras turned in all directions in search of the person who may have made the unexpected outburst, until their wearers settled a collective gaze upon the young lady who clattered down the external iron stairway in a navy blue skirt, white blouse and broad beret while holding securely onto its metal rail with one hand and vigorously waved to us with the other; a young lady who I knew more from related stories than through acquaintance. It was Millie's friend, Abbie Taylor, a member of the family who owns the mixed business where she works in Cheltenham; Horty also knows her well.

"Hi Abbie. Your voice sounds wonderful!" Horty shouted as she waved back to the only person, I consider, she had ever put on a pedestal and used to mercilessly follow around the playground at school, sometimes shadowing her back to Taylor's Auctions and Realty at the end of the day.

"Thanks, Horty – Hi lads! You look ready for a big day."

"Yeah, we're going to the long hollow first and then down to Ricketts Point, an' see if we can catch some fish – if the crowds haven't scared 'em off." I said raising my voice to remain heard as the tram moved on down to the corner of Tramway Parade, where the driver, Mr King, who occasionally gave us Mentone kids a free lift to and from school, stopped his horses to give them a short rest before they were to go on to the terminus in Beaumaris. When we reached the tram, Horty ran over to Abbie.

"Where yuh goin' to Abbie?" Horty asked as soon as she reached the rear of the tram and then stepped up beside her.

"I'm paying a visit to Miss Hyams at Mariemont. I believe she is poorly – Now, Millie tells me you have an opportunity at Cooblanna. I hope you take it up. Annette and Mips Kellerman are starting up a theatre group called the Follity Club – Everybody wants in."

Horty stepped over and whispered something into Abbie's ear, then gave her a quick hug, jumped off the steps and ran back to us boys. Shortly afterwards, Mr King cracked his whip and yelled 'Giddup there,' to his team of horses whose trace lines and swingle-tree slapped and jingled around the corner into Tramway Parade.

Before the tram had travelled out of range, Abbie shouted. "Mr King tells me old Mrs Toy is at Moyseys selling periwinkles – I hope you've brought some pennies."

Sniffle, as quick as a flash dug deep into his pockets, pulled out a penny and showed it proudly to Abbie, who then gave a short wave before making her way inside the carriage.

◄•►

"Sniffle! – Perce! – Wait up will yuh?" I called from twenty yards behind them not long after we had passed the Rush's isolated farmhouse and headed south at the long hollow to begin our slow walk through the Beaumaris Reserve. Its sandy and seldom-used track would then take us through heath and lightly wooded country until we reached the government road above Ricketts Point; expecting to see from there the well-to-do searching in rock pools on the reef or marching in throngs past brightly coloured bathing boxes on the sheltered sandy beach.

"Horty needs a pee."

Perce turned sharply around to face me, making the hook and sinker on the line of his new fishing rod come loose from an eyelet, and head in the direction of Sniffle's face.

"Bloody girls, always goin' off for a wee at school," Perce yelled angrily. Sniffle spat out a soursob and then stepped back just in time to get out of the hook's way. "Can't hold on for quids."

"Should never let girls come along on a huntin' trip."

Horty stopped whistling and then with a muffled voice fired back at Perce from twenty yards within the scrub.

"I can hear yuh, Percival," and then paused briefly to possibly adjust herself, "An' yuh better not be takin' a pee yaself today, 'cause if you are, I'm gonna rub yuh ugly scone in it."

Sniffle then cut in, using a tone that was far from his usual mealy one.

"Listen up will yuh. There's somethin' red down that track on the right … Can't make it out clear though!"

⬤•⬤

There was indeed something red lying beyond a dense clump of tea-tree, she-oak, and wattle a couple of hundred yards along what was barely a track. This area came into view and then with the slightest movement of the head was lost from sight and all of us agreed we had to find out exactly what it was. Perce led the way until his fishing rod became caught on every tea-tree branch and she-oak frond along the way, deciding by himself that the rest of the party should forge a path for him while he marched freely at the rear.

With each step towards the red object, it grew larger in size than we had expected, and with that an anticipation grew within our tiny group to discover the actual nature of what lay ahead and why in our short lives we had never heard mention of this place.

The track suddenly closed over and Sniffle, Horty, and I had to walk backwards to make any progress and allow Perce to follow. With a huge effort, we pushed past a final mass of tea-tree and sunk into a long, vast clearing of barren red soil. At its centre, stood what would have been a low tree-lined island if surrounded by water, light coloured rings evenly spaced around its girth. We brushed ourselves down, and then stood in line and in silence, pondering what we had before us.

"Whadayuh reckon it is?" Sniffle asked quietly with his hand over his mouth.

"Red dirt with a mound in the middle." Perce replied casually.

"Ain't never seen anythin' like it," Horty added.

"Me neither," I threw in and then searched for signs if anyone had frequented this place recently. I marched to the right of the expanse and saw that the island stretched out for over a hundred yards in length, not an exact oval shape but near enough.

"Where yuh goin' Loon?" Sniffle asked, sounding a bit apprehensive about anyone in our group separating from the pack at such a time and in this vicinity.

"Just havin' a look around, Sniff," I replied calmly, trying to take a bit of mystery out of our find.

I then walked to the left of the island closer to the southern end, which was of the same nature as the north, joining the rest of our party as they walked in an even line towards the outcrop.

Once reaching the edge of the island, Perce stepped forward and pressed one of his favourite fur-lined hunting boots into a smooth section of well-washed sandy loam, stepped back and studied closely the imprint it had left behind.

"It's an exact copy of the bottom of my boot. An' it felt soft goin' in."

Sniffle, Horty, and I then went up and studied the pattern.

"Perce, try a bit higher," Horty asked with a perplexed expression on her face, all of us mystified as to how a perfect copy of the sole of a boot could be made in what we thought was loose soil.

Perce pressed his left foot into a higher section and the same result was achieved.

"Well, I'll be..." Perce said stepping back onto a section

of loose gravel immediately surrounding the island. "S'like no-one's ever stepped on this hill before."

The four of us again stood in silence staring at the imprints, until Sniffle shook his head and then spoke with unexpected determination.

"Well, we can't be just lookin' at dirt all day. We're on an adventure – Who's comin' to see what's on top." He then lost all uncertainty and commenced to run up the side of the small hill at surprising speed.

I was also caught up in Sniffle's enthusiasm, not just wanting to see what was on top, but what we could see from up there or if other strange objects abound, and besides that, just wanting to have fun with my friends, something that all of us might have little time for in the future.

I ran flat out up the embankment into soil that held firm and commenced to chase down Sniffle. Perce followed suit, but in his case, just dropped his fishing rod onto the ground beside Horty.

"If yuh think I'm your slave Perce, and I'm gonna carry your fishin' rod, yuh wrong!" Horty shouted up at him, but he completely ignored her threat. I looked down at Horty expecting her to run up the hill after us but instead she stood stubbornly with her arms crossed glaring up at me with a peculiar expression on her face, one that I didn't particularly care for.

◄•►

At the highest point on the rise, Sniffle, Perce, and I climbed the bare branches of a pine tree the likes of which we had never seen before, able to see to all directions of the compass. Perce swore he could see the tower of the new Brigidine Convent in Mentone, Sniffle certain he could make out the rear of the Great Southern Hotel at Moyseys. I was sure that a line of white smoke advancing under the low sun was a train coming into Mordialloc. Finally, we all pointed to a thin line of blue, barely visible through a screen of high gums, that must be the waters of Port Philip Bay.

We continued our march on top of the island until we reached the southern end. I took a quick peek back to where we had come from, and the scattered footprints we had left behind and wondered why, beside a couple of denuded trees, only a few scraggly reeds had managed to grow on the entire surface; and what was that strange look from Horty about?

"I'm rollin' down!" Sniffle shouted unexpectedly, shaking me out of my thoughts. He took off and pushed his school satchel towards the bottom of the island where it slid softly onto the clearing. Perce and I looked at each other and immediately gave a quick nod, which was enough for us to remove our satchels and slide them down the slope where they finished side by side with Sniffle's.

Sniffle, as carefree as I had ever seen him, did an odd hop, landed awkwardly on his side, and commenced to roll his ample frame in tight rotations towards the clearing. Perce and I made no attempt to copy Sniffle's unforgettable jump, but just laid down and let gravity roll us to the bottom while letting out screams of pure joy.

"Wooee!" We shouted until finally rolling into and upending Sniffle on the edge of the red desert. Seconds later we jumped to our feet, grabbed each other's shoulders, and began to laugh our hearts out.

# Loz and Roscoe

"**WELL, AREN'T YOUSE THREE** havin' a fine and dandy time." A deep voice echoed menacingly across the clearing until fading as if swallowed whole by the nearby bush. A voice that shook Perce, Sniffle, and I out of our short-lived rapture. We forgot about brushing the russet soil from our clothing, only interested in looking to where the sound had come from.

Not ten yards from where we stood, Loz Little was standing, eyes down and undoing the straps of a satchel – Mine! Standing to his right was his sidekick, Roscoe, with his chin raised and his arms folded across his chest in an aggressive manner, an arrogant smirk on his face.

"I've known about this place for a long time, an' *nobody's* allowed to climb it." Declared Loz in an intimidating tone.

"How we s'pposed to know that, Loz?" Perce shot back, folding his arms, and puffing out his chest as a copy of Roscoe, in a poor attempt at defiance. "If we never heard of this place before."

I looked to either side of Loz and Roscoe to make sure no other members of their push were lurking in the nearby scrub ready to join in if things became willing. Fortunately, or not, we only had Loz and Roscoe to deal with.

If it came down to a fight the numbers were in our favour, although that didn't mean we had any chance of winning, and we certainly wouldn't come out of it unscathed. I even doubted whether Perce, Sniffle, and I could overcome Loz on his own.

Parents and kids talked about Loz, and openly. They said he was a half-caste – I always thought they were mean-spirited by saying that, because it made him out to be less than what he was – a whole person.

Loz was an impressive sight if seen striding around town with his swarthy skin gleaming in the sun, his body as lean as a whippet, his movements as easy and smooth as a cat, while constantly being trailed by backslapping followers. If he looked at you sideways with his dark piercing eyes it would put a chill up your spine, and the few lads who did take him on – didn't do it again. The person who got my back up though, and whom I detested more than anyone in the world, was Roscoe. He was nothing more than a snivelling rat who licked Loz's boots and had on many occasions beaten up boys younger than himself for saying they didn't like Loz.

I was wary of Loz, and for that reason, some lads thought I was afraid of him. Regardless of what they said or thought – I kept out of his way.

"Give it back, Loz," I demanded calmly, while not expecting him to comply.

"I'm a bit hungry, Loon," Loz replied and then turned to Roscoe to ask if he was hungry too, which of course he was.

"Let's have a little peek inside," Loz said feigning a curious expression on his face as he held back the leather flap and pulled out a tin can. He then lifted the sharp edge of its lid without hesitation and looked inside. "Fat worms – nice, Loon. I'll 'ave 'em – Might go fishin' later, hey Roscoe?" Loz then placed the tin on the ground.

"What else yuh got?" Loz plunged his skeletal fingers deep inside the satchel and rummaged about until suddenly stopping his search. His darting eyes gave away that he had found something interesting. He then pulled out the small jar of honey my mum had snuck in at the last minute. I took a step towards Loz, but Perce grabbed firmly onto the back of my shirt and held me in place. Loz twisted off the lid and plunged two fingers deep inside the jar and brought out a good amount of honey which he dripped onto his tongue.

"That's disgustin', Loon. Only a baby would like that," Loz said, screwing up his face and then tossing the jar to one side, which a second later hit a small rock on the edge of the clearing and broke into shards.

The disrespect he had shown the honey threw me into a rage. I tried to run at Loz, but Perce pulled me back and charged himself. Before Perce could reach Loz, Roscoe tackled him from the side, and they crashed to the ground at the base of the island. A cloud of red dust formed as they grappled for supremacy.

I ran at Loz myself, but he easily stepped aside and tripped me up. I fell elbows first onto gravel but was quickly up and able to grab one strap of my satchel. I took a quick glance back at the mound to see Sniffle frozen to the same spot where he had first stood. Loz made me pay dearly for this loss of concentration as a powerful blow landed cleanly to the side of my face thanks to his favoured right fist. The blow shook me, and I thought I heard a girl's high-pitched voice ring out, soon realizing whose it was.

"Loz, stop it!" Horty screamed. "Stop it!"

Loz and I turned briefly to face Horty, who was walking steadily towards us.

"Horty doin' yuh fightin' for yuh now, Loon?" Loz said smartly, making me throw a straight punch at his face which managed to catch and draw blood from his cheek. To my amazement, Horty then took a strong grip on the same strap that Loz held.

"Go away, Horty." Loz screamed into her face and then tried to wrench the strap from her hands, only succeeding in making Horty over-balance and fall backwards, landing heavily on her shoulders on a patch of loose sand. Loz's face suddenly became distraught. He let go of my satchel and raised his arms high into the air, shouting at me and then at Perce and Roscoe who continued to wrestle within a cloud of dust.

"The fight is over! – I did wrong – It's over!" Loz leant down and reached for Horty, but I pushed him away without resistance and then took Horty's hand and lifted her onto her feet and away from Loz.

"I didn't mean it, Horty. I'm sorry for what I done."

"I'm good, Loz. Don't worry about that little fall," said Horty calmly as she brushed sand from her shoulders and lower arms, then showed him her elbows and hands. "See, no blood – all my fault, shouldn't a' stepped in."

"Don't matter, Horty – I did wrong."

Loz then marched over to where Roscoe and Perce held each other in a headlock, neither willing to relent even as both their mouths blew dust up from just above the ground.

"Let him go, Roscoe." With that Loz leant down and grabbed Roscoe forcibly by the arm and commenced to drag him along the ground until he let go of Perce.

Loz then lifted Roscoe onto his feet in one strong motion and pushed him stumbling towards the nearest scrub. Halfway across the small desert, we could hear Loz say.

"We never hurt girls."

—•—

Nobody knew what to say after the fight. We went silently about dusting ourselves down, checking our elbows and knees for cuts and scratches, and our clothes for rips. My jaw was tender to the touch and hard to open, and

I wondered what would have happened if Horty hadn't stepped in. Perce spat sand out onto the clearing and then wiped his mouth. Horty lowered her head and shook twigs and leaves out from her hair, before flicking it backwards and retying it into the loose and curly bundle it was before the fight. Appearing deep in thought, she adjusted the golden ribbon on her straw hat and pressed the hat firmly back onto her head.

"Just knew Loz was a sap," Sniffle said as a brazen statement, his feet still rooted to the same spot as before the fight. "Yuh got him a good one, Loon. I never heard of anyone drawin' blood on Loz before – I'm gonna tell everyone he's a real sap."

"Shut up Sniffle – You wouldn' dare say that to Loz's face, so don't start sayin' it now!" Perce snapped as he kicked at the sandy gravel only managing to cover his boots thicker in red dust. I stared back along the length of the island and was astounded how quickly we had sullied its smooth, pristine surface. Loz was right, we should have left it alone.

"This place is givin' me the creeps," I said quietly, noticing how quickly an eerie silence had returned to our immediate surrounds. "We should go."

"Go home, yuh sayin'?" Perce took a step closer to me, a degree of anger still left in him.

"Never said that, but if yuh wanna make somethin' of it – I will," I also took a step forward, not willing to put up with any of Perce's nonsense, and just angry about how our adventure had started off so badly and looked ready to fail at the first obstacle.

"Stop it, will youse two!" Horty screamed and then stepped in between us. "My dad's missus was right when she said men don't need no excuse to start a fight – We only left home two hours ago an' yuh wanna face up for a second round."

Bewildering as it was to hear Horty agreeing with anything Lizbeth had said, she was right. We never wanted our day to be like this, and so soon. As a welcome distraction, Sniffle let out a small cough from behind us, and then another. Unsure of what was ailing him, we all turned to look.

"Sorry, I got scared before – but I couldn't move my feet to help," Sniffle said while bending forward, gripping his shorts by the cuffs, and trying to lift his feet from their fixed position.

"Still can't. Can yuh give me a hand?"

Without prompting, Perce and I walked to either side of Sniffle and placed one hand under his arm and one around his back. Horty stepped in front of him.

"Sniff, I saw yuh doin' a great hop before yuh rolled down the hill,"

She then stepped to the side. "Just do it again."

"On three," I called out. "One – two – three!"

Perce and I tensed our shoulders to take Sniffle's weight, but no sooner had we commenced to lift than Sniffle strode forward and immediately went over and picked up his satchel.

"Can we get goin' now?"

# CHAPTER EIGHT

## In 'The Sunny South'

HORTY WALKED A GOOD ten yards in front of me, Sniffle shuffled along a couple of yards to her side. A couple of yards behind me, I could hear Perce kick at the gravel of the reserve's rough track, obviously still feeling aggrieved by recent events. It was only mid-morning, and our group was no longer marching side by side with excitement but dragging itself along like a defeated rabble on a back road that had thankfully begun to descend to its conclusion and our destination: Ricketts Point.

As Perce continued to kick at the track, I wondered what in his life had made him like he was; often sullen and hard to get on with. At school he kept to himself having few mates to speak of, which made it even more of a surprise that he had chummed up so quickly with Sniffle. He spent most of his free time out on his own shooting the dwindling local wildlife or on rare occasions with his host of brothers up to mischief out in the bush or down by the bay, giving his tormented and only sister Kate, and his long-suffering mother, a breather.

Perce's dad was only seen around Mentone every three or four months, buying up big on his return from working a mine near Bairnsdale. A large and ruddy-faced man, his brag and bluster in public made most children and adults prefer to walk on the other side of the road. At home he was reported to be a tyrant, saying hello to the children only once on arrival, who in haste fled the house, and then giving them a solitary cold goodbye when he left.

Out of the blue Sniffle piped up, perhaps sick of the gloom that had engulfed us.

"I got somethin' funny to tell yuh!" Everybody pulled up to gawk at Sniffle, glad someone had broken the silence.

"Well..." Sniffle hesitated and then burst forth, "My mum and dad still have a bath together – just like kids – an' blow bubbles an' throw suds at each other."

Horty and I burst out laughing, whereas Perce seemed to think carefully through what Sniffle had said.

"Never gonna see *my* folks do that!" He said to our continuing delight. Sniffle's face then went blank as he focused on something down the track.

We turned to see two gents too formally dressed for this isolated bush location, wandering up the track towards us carrying bulging leather cases strapped with correspondence as if on their way to an office in the city. The younger of the two, a heavily moustached and more lightly dressed man was toking on a rummy cigar that could be smelt from their distance of twenty-five yards. The elder wore a bowler hat and fob watch, while exuding the reserve of a man who spent his days locked in a dusty office scratching down a mountain of numbers.

Curiously, the two men paid us little attention until they reached within yards, seemingly only interested in the surrounding scrub. The men then suddenly stopped and looked us up and down.

"Hello children!" The younger man said in a commanding tone, "You look like you've been in the wars."

Our small troupe went silent, not expecting to encounter these types.

Perce then raised his chin and replied defiantly, "We're not children and we held our own."

"Pleased to hear that..." The younger man replied with little concern either way, then aimed his pointer down the lane. "Do any of you young chaps or young lady know who lives further along this stretch? – We can pay a penny or two for that knowledge."

Quick as a flash Perce's eyes lit up. "A penny each would be better," he said turning to Horty, Sniffle and I for our approval, which we gave.

"Then we are agreed." The younger man likewise receiving a nod from his older partner.

Perce still grinning from the windfall coming our way, puffed out his chest, swung his long arm around and pointed towards Cheltenham.

"Well, the Darlings are right down the end of the track, on

the far side of the main road. Balcombe Road that is. On the left before that there's heath and open country that becomes a swamp when it rains. The McDonalds and Rushs have farms nearby and the Wells are closer to Mentone, where we're from," Perce then pointed in the general direction of Mentone.

"There are also some fine houses closer to the bay."

The younger man scribbled down the names and drew rough diagrams in a notebook.

"Were you planning a spot of fishing today, or have you already caught some?" The older man asked while studying the flex and sway of the long fishing rod attached to Perce's satchel.

"None yet," Perce emphasised, "We're going to find a good spot later on somewhere along the rock shelves." Perce waved his arm in an arc to where the shelves would have been if not hidden by thick bush.

The two men then spoke quietly to each other.

"Do any one of you know the owner of this immediate area, a Mr Dalgetty?" The younger man asked, the skin above the high stiff collar of his white shirt, glowing red the longer he stood in the brightening sun. He had a glance at each of us.

"What sort of man is he?"

"I seen him when I was younger, at the local produce in Mentone," I said half-heartedly, beginning to dislike the nature of this man's questioning, "... and *everybody* speaks well of him." A wave of dizziness then came over me as I rested my jaw.

"He must be quite old now, I would a' thought." Perce added to have the final say.

"He hasn't done a lot to improve his land." The younger man added as he broke a twig off a giant coastal banksia on the city side of the track.

"Doesn't have to..." Horty shot back, perhaps feeling a twinge of protectiveness for a local not here to defend himself. The younger man swung around to give an annoyed glare, which soon mellowed to a smile and a nod, perhaps appreciating her frankness.

"So, the land through here is all like this, lightly wooded with sand and scrub?" He enquired further, continuing to peer in the direction of Cheltenham.

"There's a funny red desert in the bush up on the left – and a decent island in the middle." Bragged Perce as if he had discovered it like Captain Cook.

"Indeed!" the older man stated with interest. "Is this island made of rock?" His expression hardening as he mouthed out and totted up numbers as if its sheer existence was costing him money.

"No, it's like soft sand." Perce replied to the older man's relief.

"Could you take us to this desert?" the younger man asked with some assurance that we would.

"No, we can't!" I replied swiftly, leaving no doubt that I for one would not be going back. Horty, Perce, and Sniffle shook their heads as well. The two gents again spoke quietly, the younger man accepting our reluctance with 'that's fine'.

"Well, we will say farewell then and continue under our own steam." The younger man said as he produced four pennies which he gave to Perce to distribute. As the gents bent down to pick up their cases, Sniffle asked politely.

"D'yuh want somethin' tuh drink before yuh go? – It's a decent walk."

The gentlemen nodded in agreement, then we found the perfect spot under the limp fronds of a russet she-oak for Sniffle to produce from his satchel an old beer bottle filled with water. The men insisted Horty had a drink first, before each of us took a swig in turn.

"Have you, young folk, ever seen a horseless carriage, or an auto car or motor car as they are often referred?" the younger man asked with a degree of levity, as if we perhaps lived too far beyond the realms of civilisation.

I shook my head only ever seeing a steam tractor, then looked quizzically over to my friends. Perce put up his hand.

"Yeah, I caught a glimpse of a motored cycle once, as it ran beside the railway tracks near home." Perce said describing an incident that I had never heard mention of before, "... smelt like kerosene."

"It most likely was running on it," the older man stated, "I believe that kerosene or a petroleum derivative will be the preferred accelerant to decide the final design of the engine." He then produced a handkerchief from his pocket, lifted his hat and wiped his brow. "...of course, the populace will have the final say,"

"The general public have generally shown a lack of forethought in the past, always opting for the least arduous option." The younger man responded on a subject of which I had limited knowledge. "Electricity is the future for me. The lead and acid battery has been available for quite a while now and the attached motor produces little offensive odour and no horrendous noise."

The older man then threw his arms up in the air.

"But those batteries that you are so much in favour of, are of a prohibitive price and a great difficulty to charge." The two men then decided to study either up or down the track. Perce looked at me with bewilderment, also struggling to follow their conversation.

"Don't think any sort of carriage, motorised or not, could get through this sandy old track," I threw in only to break the silence.

The two gentlemen then studied up the track and the build-up of sand which had swamped several sections of the lane. The men then went to pick up their cases.

"I'd like to thank each of you for your time and especially you, young man for sharing your water," the older man touched the brim of his hat towards Sniffle. "I think my associate and I can agree on one thing – sometimes the obvious can be right in front of your nose."

The two men then began to march north, still debating

the best way forward for the motor car.

"The challenge in the future may not be the type of vehicle in use," The younger man's words fading into the distance, "...but what form of tyre allows it to cross a multitude of surfaces."

Without delay, we picked up our satchels and continued our trek south.

※

Perce with newfound enthusiasm reached the government road above Ricketts Point before Horty, Sniffle, and I, who were happy to dawdle behind and take in the mysterious cracking and whispering sounds coming from deep within the nearby scrub as it became flooded by the warm morning sun. Overhead, flocks of birds swirled in a light breeze that grew stronger with each step we took closer to the bay.

We met up with Perce at the exposed tram tracks that ran down the centre of the coastal road, in one direction towards Cheltenham, the other Sandringham. On the Cheltenham side, the tracks left the bay and turned into the lower section of Tramway Parade, where they weaved through tall trees, roughly hewn holiday cabins, scattered tents, and the odd grand home, until reaching the main terminus at Bodley Street, situated conveniently at only a short walk from the Great Southern Hotel and the esplanade above Beaumaris Bay.

"Ave a look over there!" Sniffle shouted while standing tiptoes on a rail and pointing over tea-tree and she-oak to small groups of brightly dressed adults and children scrambling over tidal reefs that extended out into the bay from the gleaming sands of Ricketts Point beach.

"Heaps of people out on the rocks."

Perce with a dubious expression on his face stepped beside Sniffle to see for himself if there was indeed 'heaps'. Feeling a light tug on my sleeve I turned to see Horty gazing down the rails that led towards Sandringham.

Three hundred yards away, two trams packed with passengers above and inside, wheeled around the final bend before Ricketts Point. As the line straightened, the trams' drivers pulled back hard on their steed's reins, the horses with manes flying, snorted and huffed to a halt along a low section of the coastal road not two hundred yards from the sparkling waters of Port Philip Bay.

"There y'are Perce!" Sniffle exclaimed with eyes agog, "Toffs by the dozen!"

Perce nodded his satisfaction.

Wanting at all costs to get to the trams as quickly as possible, we decided to ditch our satchels and fishing gear under a large melaleuca bush and run downhill at full stride, so we would be able to reach the resting trams in time to greet their large number of passengers as they stepped down from the spiral stairwells onto the sand and gravel beside the tracks.

—•—

"Hello, how was your trip?" Horty politely asked a young lady wearing a white crocheted dress who was clunking down the iron steps in high-sided boots. The lady returned a nod and a smile before whispering something to a rakish man in front of her.

"Get a good view from up there?" Perce asked two well-dressed gentlemen who he may have been hoping would turn out to be as generous as the last two.

"Bet yuh can see for miles!" I called to a woman urging her children to exit the roof's yellow bench seats, a call which went unanswered. All of us trying to engage with the well-heeled travellers, for no other reason than to see what they were like, how they dressed, how they spoke, or anything about them that was different. Most passengers however, paid us no mind, only interested in making their way towards the beach in rough Indian files as quickly as possible.

"Push off, you little rascals." One tram driver snarled at us through gnashing yellow teeth and then with a sweep of his Derby hat over our ducking heads, made us take several steps away from the tram.

Sniffle by this time had attached himself to a toffee-nosed

boy in a sailor suit with bucket and spade in hand; a beak-nosed nanny following behind, protected him alone from the bright sun with her frilled parasol. Sniffle like an experienced guide, directing them west to a more secluded section of Ricketts Point.

Horty, already a good way along the main path that skirted the beach, was making herself useful to a young family of four, who were overloaded with picnic baskets, rugs, and a large umbrella. Their youngest, a lively boy, was having his shirt stretched to ripping point by his mother to prevent him from running recklessly towards the foreshore; while the father was having his own struggle with a disinterested daughter, refusing to enjoy the day.

With most of the new arrivals having already dispersed to the beach. Perce and I gave up any further attempts to engage and headed towards the reefs to enjoy the day like everybody else.

⋅◆⋅

# CHAPTER NINE

# Frozen in Time

AT THE FURTHEST MARGIN of the larger of the two main sandstone reefs jutting out from Ricketts Point beach, Perce and I peered curiously over the ragged edge of its widest and deepest rock pool; the giggles of children and chattering of adults wafting over to us from the small groups of recently arrived passengers who maintained a safe distance from the slippery algae-covered surface we were on. There was no need to ask any of the children scouring the rock pools and nearby beach what they were looking for – we were all after the same thing – Shells! – and the larger and more colourful the better.

I had never seen the waters of the bay so flat and still as they were now, and not a breath of wind disturbed the glassy surface of the foot deep pool we were leaning over on hands and knees. Within its walls were brown-streaked mussels, spiky purple urchins, and bulbous clumps of seaweed clinging to rock ledges or wedged into crevices; dozens of tiny colourful shells of strange and interesting shapes lay scattered across its ragged floor. Nevertheless, there was a greater prize I was after, and one few would expect to find in this vicinity: a conch shell. And although my parents had found a good specimen on the beach below the slopes years ago. I wanted one of my own.

Perce and I hadn't seen Sniffle or Horty since they had befriended their respective passengers over half an hour ago, but it didn't matter, all my friends were now part of the same wonder and excitement that the people who had paid good money and travelled a long distance must be feeling: the unhurried calmness of the beach on a magnificent day.

I surveyed the scene from the quiet slopes closer to Sandringham through to the serene setting of families forming circles on picnic rugs under the welcome shade of she-oaks and banksias opposite the reef. Panning further to my right, I noticed at the bathing boxes closest to Table Rock Point, a small but lively crowd gathered around a tall man who was adjusting and manoeuvring a strange form of equipment into place. On the edge of the crowd, I could pick out Horty with her recently acquired family, holding the hand of their disinterested daughter.

However, all the commotion in front of the bathing boxes was distracting me from my main objective; to find a conch. I left the rock pool and Perce and headed to the far end of the rocky outcrop. I cautiously hopped my way over to its edge, laid down, leant far over the side, and had a good peek into any cave or shelter that souvenir hunters may have overlooked. Sure enough, there was an object with thin, curved, and bony points jutting out from the sand that could easily have been the outer fringes of a conch. I stretched and extended my right hand down to its limit, just managing to grab a point when.

"Octopus!" Sniffle and Perce screamed out in unison from behind and above me. I pulled my hand back with unjustified fear; my elbows and forearms digging into rock as they lifted me in panic away from what turned out to be nothing more than the skeleton of a small animal. I rolled over to see Perce and Sniffle shaking each other's hands and almost crying with laughter.

"You bloody buggers!" I shouted without caring who heard.

"You're a scaredy cat, Loon – an' yuh can't deny it." Perce said with a grin and then pointed down at my shorts. "...an' yuh wet yuh pants, too."

I looked immediately down to see that I had without noticing lain in a small well in the rock, and the crotch of my shorts had become soaked to the skin. To add injury to insult I had blood running down my scratched arms. I squatted and cupped water in my hand from a rock pool and commenced to wash the crusting blood away.

"Why yuh back here for, anyway, Sniffle," I asked sarcastically, annoyed at being caught off guard. "Where's yuh toffee mate and his nanny?"

"Too much of a skite that kid." Sniffle fired back, not caring if I was happy or not. "He topped me on everythin' I said."

"I told him I got three good agates – he said he had a bag full of all-sorts. My dad wants tuh have a ride in a motor car – his dad owns one. He even said he'd caught a giant octopus, when I said we were goin' fishin'."

A cheer went up from the crowd around the tall man and our attention was draw to what may be creating all the fuss.

"Forget about the shells," I said disappointedly. "There's none left here anyway. Let's see what's goin' on with the tall fella on the beach."

⟶•⟵

When Perce, Sniffle, and I arrived in front of the bathing boxes, Horty was still with the family she had met earlier and still holding the hand of their daughter. The pig-tailed girl was showing a great interest in the deft manoeuvres of the tall and surprisingly young man standing alternatively behind or in front of what I knew from Fairlam's photography shop in Cheltenham to be a bellows camera; its extended and brilliantly polished wood and brass frame held steadily in place by a matching tripod stand pushed firmly into sand.

Covering and then uncovering himself with a wide black cloth attached to the rear of the camera, the hatless and rosy cheeked young man called a waiting group of three elderly women forward. The unaccompanied women, who were surely close friends chatted at a rapid rate and were exuding great excitement as they moved forward unsteadily across loose sand to the firmer lower section of the beach, their heavily beaded dresses and wide floral hats a hindrance to every movement.

"That is a good distance for me, thank you ladies." The young man said in an accomplished and surprisingly deep voice, causing the ladies to hush, form a line and face towards the camera. The young man made an adjustment which lifted the camera at the front, then disappeared once again under the dark cloth.

"Now ladies, it may be preferable to *not* focus on the lens in front to the camera, but perhaps above my left shoulder to the wonders of the bay beyond." The photographer said upon resurfacing and taking hold of the cap over the lens and gripping something unseen to the rear of the camera.

"Also, before I remove the plate from its slide and the cap from the lens, I will require *no* movement." The young man then spoke to the milling crowd.

"Ladies and gentlemen, if you don't mind, may I have a clear space behind my subjects?"

The tall photographer once again disappeared under the cover as the enthralled crowd withdrew only yards. The young man then stretched the bellow an inch forward, and a touch more until he was happy, a dark plate was subsequently slid out and held up. A hush went over the crowd who held their breath to wish a good outcome for the three ladies. The young man then removed the brass lens cover for a fixed time and after a further interval poked his head out from beneath the black cloth.

"Ladies, I believe we have success." The young photographer said to a polite round of applause from the crowd and the three ladies themselves. He subsequently removed a substantial cartridge from the rear box of the camera and secured it within the dark confines of a solid leather suitcase.

"Ladies, thank you for your custom and stay nearby to discuss delivery arrangements."

Horty left her young family who were to have their picture taken next and pushed in beside Perce, Sniffle, and I, not two yards to the side from where the young photographer was concentrating his thoughts on the following job at hand. He cleaned lenses, tightened and secured parts, and put other mysterious objects into place, all apparently necessary to capture a flawless portrait.

"Do you like takin' pictures?" Sniffle asked the young man a touch daftly.

"What's not to like." He replied politely while reaching for a leather pouch beside the tripod.

Perce rubbed his head trying to think up a better question than Sniffle's.

"How much coin do yuh make outta each picture?"

"There are too many variables to be certain, but enough to allow me to travel regularly and have all my expenses paid." The photographer then stood at his tallest and smiled heartily at Perce, assuring him that there was indeed 'coin' in it. "I hope to travel to Philip Island next week for an extended stay."

The young man looked at Horty and me in turn with the expectation of further questions.

"Well, if there is nothing more – I shall proceed to the family waiting patiently."

The tall man then waved decisively for the young family to come towards him, just in advance of giving our group a subtle backhand wave to go away.

No sooner had we stepped back to the foreshore, than Horty crouched down and began to undo the laces of her sand covered shoes.

"My feet are killin' me – I'm gettin' out of these shoes for a while."

Heads were nodded in unison, and shortly after shoes, boots, and socks were ripped off and red and sore feet plunged into cool water, the relief visible on our faces as we worked our toes into the oozing sand at the edge of the foreshore. There the four of us stood contentedly watching an excited young girl and her family pose happily in front of a hushed crowd and an ingenious young photographer.

◆•◆

## CHAPTER TEN

# Old Mrs Toy

MRS TOY WAS EXACTLY where Abbie Taylor said she would be, close by the cliffs at Moysey's old house block, which was conveniently located opposite the entrance to Bodley Street and in full view of the animated comings and goings of the well-healed as they strolled along the esplanade above Beaumaris Bay or in the forecourt of the prestigious Great Southern Hotel.

In the shadow of a pine tree, Mrs Toy in a stained red and gold apron was leaning over a steaming cast-iron cauldron and using a hand-fashioned wire net to retrieve round bleached-white shells from within its boiling water. She then rolled them like a bowling ball into a high-edged wooden tray held securely over her shrunken shoulders and hunched back by leather straps.

Mrs Toy was somewhat of a mysterious character in the area, no-one certain of her background, her age, or even where she resided. Rumours abounded that she had been the promised child bride to an old and powerful mandarin in a remote region of China, saved from this fate by a German missionary who secreted her out of the country, only to die of dysentery himself on their voyage to Australia. All this gossip likely coming from people with fanciful minds and nothing better to do.

Suddenly Mrs Toy's alert brown eyes shifted under her frayed straw hat, noticing the approach of a well-dressed family of four crossing the esplanade road, either intrigued by the steaming cauldron or tempted by the scent of the salty molluscs within her tray. To further entice the family to step under the cooling foliage of the pine, she poured a dash of vinegar over each shell.

◆•◆

No sooner had our small group stepped out from a coastal path and onto the esplanade and Sniffle had noticed Mrs Toy than he raced ahead of us in a beeline towards her.

"Mrs Toy! Mrs Toy!" Sniffle wheezed, short of breath as he shot past the family's two identically dressed daughters who pulled up abruptly. Sniffle with chest heaving, stood in front of Mrs Toy, and had a quick peruse of the shells as they rolled about in the wooden tray before saying. "Can I have a penny's worth of winkles?" Taken aback, Mrs Toy said through pursed lips.

"Wait your turn, rude boy," Then waved Sniffle away with her wire net. "You push in on those girls. Go back to your friends and get some manners."

Sniffle, reluctantly and with his head down shuffled over to where Horty, Perce, and I had placed our retrieved satchels and rods under the canopy of the pine tree. Forming a circle we quietly chuckled to ourselves about Sniffle's indulgent behaviour and Mrs Toy's wild brandishing of a wire net.

The father of the two girls, unmissable in matching white pants, jacket, and pith hat, was also enjoying Sniffle's performance. He went over and placed his arms over his daughters' shoulders, where he was soon joined by their mother in an equally striking white dress and broad floral hat. This lady then whispered softly into her husband's ear to which he nodded and gained the attention of Mrs Toy by coughing into his hand.

"Madame, this young man," The father said pointing to Sniffle, "is obviously in urgent need of sustenance and who are we, strangers to this locale, to deny him this small want." The lady in the floral hat turned her attention away from Mrs Toy to judge the reaction of Sniffle at being given his own way, which was quite positive.

"Madame, our daughters are happy to wait." The mother said as she returned her focus to Mrs Toy.

Mrs Toy her hand shaking in annoyance waved her net at Sniffle and then begrudgingly said. "Come on then, hurry up. I get your winkles."

Sniffle was about to jump to his feet, when Horty grabbed Sniffle by one arm, and I took the other, at the same time as Perce rolled about in hysterics behind his newfound friend.

"Let me go! – Let me go will yuhs!" Sniffle demanded, wriggling his hardest to try to break free.

Horty whispered in his ear, "Let the girls go first."

"No!" Sniffle sneered back defiantly. Perce then sat up no longer finding Sniffle's stubbornness funny.

"C'mon Sniffle, let the girls go first?" He asked as a plea.

"No!" Sniffle repeated even louder. Without delay, Perce covered his mouth with his long, skinny hands and spoke to the parents of the waiting family.

"Our friend Neville here, would like nothing more than to let your daughters go first."

With Sniffle unable to complain, both parents gave a nod of gratitude in his direction and let their daughters go over to Mrs Toy, who had already prepared two bags of periwinkles for them. The girls handed over their pennies which were quickly shoved deep into her apron pocket. As soon as the young family had left, Mrs Toy waved us over. However, she would have to wait for all our orders, as Sniffle had immediately upon being released, stormed off in a huff to the nearby lookout.

◆·◆

Sniffle eventually got his periwinkles and caught up with the rest of us in no time. With barely a word spoken between us, we picked out and chewed down the curly morsels until a pile of empty shells had formed in the centre of our circle. Satisfied and ready to leave, we decided to ask Mrs Toy if she knew of any good fishing spots on this side of Table Rock.

"Next to the rock," she said rapidly as she served two more well-dressed children from her seemingly endless supply of periwinkles, "Nobody go there."

We thanked Mrs Toy for her advice and tasty wares and then stepped out from under the pine's foliage into blinding sunlight, only to be stopped after a few yards.

"If you hot, there's an inlet near the old harbour, very quiet ... I get my winkles there." Mrs Toy then put a finger up to her lips, to ensure we kept this our secret.

We waved our appreciation and then proceeded south towards Table Rock, leaving behind a lady who under different circumstances may have been the reluctant wife of a rich mandarin, to serve a steady line-up of well-to-do customers.

—•—

# CHAPTER ELEVEN

# By Hook or by Crook

**THE SUN WAS DIRECTLY** above our heads and powerful enough to make us stay under the thick foliage of the manna, swamp, and red gums scattered along the coastal path we tramped upon, on our way to find the perfect fishing spot on the Beaumaris Bay side of Table Rock Point.

The further we descended towards the waters of the bay, the thicker the ground covering of tea-tree and vines became until it closed over our path completely and forced us to climb over and around matts of entangled bushes. Finally, we were able to reach a clearing in front of a low rock shelf which lay beside the imposing red and brown edifice of Table Rock.

Once upon the low shelf, Perce, Sniffle, and I had to negotiate a thick covering of green and slippery seaweed bulbs, intermittently dispersed sharp edged rockpools, and randomly scattered rocks before we were able to reach the shelf's ragged end and the bay beyond. There we got to work spacing out our fishing lines at ten even paces: worms wriggling irresistibly on hooks only a foot below the surface.

When we had finished securing our lines, we stepped back over the plateau to a small shell grit and sand beach at its rear where we had left Horty earlier after she had complained of feeling dizzy because of the increasing heat. After a brief search we found her curled up fast asleep under the leaves of a melaleuca bush; her arms covering her face, her legs pulled up within her skirt.

We left Horty in peace and made ourselves comfortable on the grit and sand beach and began to watch our lines. We drew figures with sticks in the sand and watched our lines, laid on our sides while brushing sandflies away and watched our lines, wiped our soaked necks free of perspiration and watched our lines. The temperature now was oppressive with waves of heat rolling off the exposed shelf before us. The best we could do was cover our faces with our shirts, leaving our torsos to the mercy of sandflies and midges.

Sniffle then suddenly looked up, got to his feet and ran and hopped towards his homemade handline which he had jammed tightly into a crack at the edge of the rock shelf. A few steps before the end of the plateau he stopped, knelt, and began a slow crawl over bulbs of seaweed until he was able to peek over the edge to the water below. Sniffle then withdrew a yard, turned back to Perce and me, put a finger up to his lips and signalled for us to come over while keeping our heads down.

Perce, however, shook his head and returned it under the

cover of his shirt while groaning as if sick.

"You go Loon. It's too hot out there."

*Bet you won't wait for the fish to go cold after we cook it for yuh Perce!* I shook my head at his unending foibles.

Maintaining my balance, I slipped over hidden cracks and pools, kept my head down as best possible, and then crawled up to the end of the rock ledge within a couple of yards to the side of Sniffle and peered cautiously over the edge. At that point the floor of the bay appeared void of water, drained dry by a massive tide, leaving only fields of rippled sand between patches of vibrant green seagrass. The only thing that gave away the presence of water was a sizeable fish with bright silver scales and large, round yellow eyes winding its way through a sandy gully in the direction of a fissure in the rock ledge where the baited hook at the end of Sniffle's line was floating free.

Stealthily, Sniffle slid his hand over, gripped his fishing line and then mouthed something at me that could have been, 'Let me go, the fish is taking its time.'

I shook my head at that, screwed up my face and put my hand up to make Sniffle stop. By this time, he had produced an angry look and mouthed something like, 'Let me know where the fish tucks the twine!'

I screwed up my face again and whispered, "Wha'?"

Sniffle got to his knees and shouted, "Let me know when the fish takes the bloody line!"

Sniffle and I then immediately looked down to see the

fish, its tail beating at a rate, race in a suicidal attempt to get the worm it desired. I whispered.

"Wait, wait…" and then cried, "Now!"

Sniffle pulled as hard as he could on his fraying horse-hair line which was wound through a maze of cracks and sharp edges until it went taut just as the mouth of the desperate fish gobbed the hook and worm in one go. Sniffle now standing gave a sharp tug on his line and with a huge heave flung the fish away from its aquatic home and onto the steaming plateau behind. Out of the corner of my eye I noticed Perce slipping over the shelf towards us.

*Piss off Perce!*

"Wha'd yuh get lads?" he shouted excitedly.

"Well, it's got big yellow eyes, so it must be a yelloweye." Sniffle replied smartly, shaking his head as I had done earlier.

The fish, acutely aware of its predicament thrashed and flopped about on the rock shelf until falling fortuitously into a shallow rock pool. Out of nowhere a slim white hand came down and picked the fish up in one clean motion before another hand bludgeoned the back of its head with the help of a small cast iron frypan. Seconds later, Horty with knife in hand commenced to gut the fish.

"We're gonna need some hot coals to cook this oily old yellaeye." She stated calmly.

—•—

I watched Horty as she nonchalantly flung the bones of the oily yet filling yelloweye into the bay and then poured water over the ashes of the small fire we had set safely out at the end of the shelf. She then returned to where Perce, Sniffle and I were sitting on the sand and shell grit beach and stood before us with hands on hips like a disgruntled school mistress.

"Yuh know yuh gotta wait half an hour after lunch 'fore yuh can go swimmin'," 

Perce, Sniffle, and I nodded in agreement.

"An' just 'cause yuh *can* go swimmin' doesn't mean the good people visitin' here today wanna see yuh bare behinds and wrinkly bits while yuh doin' it." Horty then wriggled her pointer at us, "So, can yuh do 'em a favour an' keep your doodles in yuh drawers?"

Perce, Sniffle, and I nodded in agreement.

◀•▶

Of course, we had no intention of paying any mind to Horty's request to not swim in our natural state. How could we after the success of catching our lunch on such a sweltering day when there was the reward of cool water waiting afterwards. We waited until Horty had stepped out of sight around the low rocks of the shoreline in search of Mrs Toy's hidden inlet, then we followed an almost over-grown path that extended over the back of Table Rock and used worn footmarks to reach the rear of the ancient sandstone pillar; thankfully deserted of anyone who might find our normal summer pastime a tad unsavoury.

Perce, Sniffle, and I stepped over volcanic rings set for millennia in the rock's surface until coming to an abrupt halt at its ragged edge, where we could peer down upon water without ripple or current. From there the marine world stretched out into the bay as patches of intermittent sand, vegetation, and stone; the only discernible movement a packet steamer on the horizon proceeding at full speed towards Hobsons Bay.

"Now Sniff, y'are gonna jump in aren't yuh?" I asked on noticing his eyes widen and transfix on the drop that he would soon have to accomplish. After no response, Perce added tersely.

"Yuh promised 'fore we came up here that you'd jump. So yuh'd betta not chicken out now!"

"I'm not chickenin' out," Sniffle grumped back, "I just can't see the water, that's all." An uncertainty growing on his face.

"Well, I'm jumpin' in on my own if yuh gonna squib it," Perce declared while bending down and undoing the laces of his boots, "It's too bloody hot out here!"

I didn't want to appear to be a squib either, so I leant down and began to undo my shoelaces as well. However, Sniffle was still unmoved and continued to stare over the edge at the glassy surface below, until thankfully a solitary seagull landed nearby and waded across our proposed landing spot, showing clearly that there was indeed plenty of water to plunge into.

"I'm gonna do it," Sniffle said with resolve and then began to undo his laces, "but I gotta do it now or else I'm not gonna do it at all!"

"Rightio, let's get our clobber off then." Perce said with exasperation, eager to get this jump done.

We made for the side of the rock above our grit and sand beach and frantically ripped off shoes and socks, shirts and shorts, until we were left with only our underpants on. Glancing occasionally at each other's pale and shaking bodies we quickly lowered our drawers as one, gathered our clothes together and threw them over the side of Table Rock where they landed in a scattered heap near our secluded fishing spot.

Satisfied there were no prying eyes in the vicinity, we quickly returned to the centre of the rock, took a deep breath and then without indecision sprinted in a line across the primeval stone before flinging ourselves out and over the edge into mid-air; our legs turning like pedals on an invisible bicycle, our arms flapping like helpless wings, our lungs screaming to the heavens. Steeling my body for the chill to come, I slipped into cool water, leaving behind wispy towers of bubbles that fizzed quickly to the surface.

I searched in all directions for Perce and Sniffle to assure myself they were fine, until their faces appeared before my blurring eyes, then we strove to climb the short distance to find air.

Sniffle and I burst out of the water together both inhaling large gulps of air. Shortly afterwards, Perce burst out but instead of taking a breath howled out a loud 'Wooee' and punched the water with exhilaration. I shivered as a tingle ran through my body, so happy to be alive at that very moment.

# CHAPTER TWELVE

# Hidden Pool

ecro

PERCHED HIGH ON STAINED white rocks, a flock of gannets looked warily down upon me as I pulled up and treaded water at the entrance to what I assumed to be Mrs Toy's secluded inlet. I looked around for Horty while taking in deep breaths after intermittently walking and swimming from our makeshift camp. I found her standing ankle deep in water on the edge of the inlet searching through stones and shells with only her singlet and petticoat on.

"Hey!" I waved and called out enthusiastically to Horty, who took her time then looked up with disdain.

"I know you boys went swimmin' in the raw!" Horty shouted and then threw shells angrily at the water, "I could hear yuh screamin' – it's not nice lookin' from a girl's point of view."

Silenced, I glided up to and sat cautiously on a submerged rock ledge that had formed in a semi-circle around a natural bathing pool, a large swirl of seagrass at its centre. I thought through a reply.

"It's nice and cool in here – ain't it Hort?"

"Yuh don't have tuh change the subject, every time I say somethin' yuh don't like, Loon." Horty snapped back and kicked water in my direction, "That's what milksops do."

*Bloody hell, Hort! What's got on your goat?*

I was about to swear at Horty for the first time in my life, then I thought it might be better if I fired back a few volleys myself.

"Listen here, Horty Brown. I'll swim how I want – So keep yuh nose out of it!" I said while splashing water in her direction. "An' I do have shorts on!"

After a brief silence Horty replied apologetically.

"Sorry, Loon, yuh know I don't think you're a milksop – it's just..."

I knew being thrown to the ground by Loz would have shaken Horty up, but her behaviour today was at times odd. All I could think of was that she was annoyed at her stepmother for wanting to pack her off to one girls' school or another. All of which wasn't my fault, however it was still better to make light of this situation.

"Remember how we used to have baths together as kids, just like Sniffle's mum and dad do now," Horty looked at me curiously and reluctantly nodded her head, "Yeah..."

"Remember you used to blow bubbles all the time?" Horty nodded her head and seemed to know what I was about to say, "...from yuh bum!"

Horty couldn't prevent a giggle slipping out and then

with a grin raised her hands to display a variety of objects.

"Look what I found – heaps of nice shells – and even got a big shark's tooth." Horty then walked over and put the assortment in a pile next to her shirt and skirt which were lying safely on a shelf above the water line.

Expecting Horty to put her clothes back on and head back to camp, I was surprised when she walked back into the water until waist deep and then stretched out her arms and glided over to where I was sitting on the rock ledge. Seconds later she was sitting beside me stretching her legs out into the pool.

"What's Sniffle and Perce up to?"

"Drownin' worms…" I replied leaning back and stretching out my legs as well, "Won't be much happenin' till the tide changes."

Without allowing time to settle, Horty pushed off from the ledge and swam towards the seagrass, her white singlet and petticoat rippling over her slim body and pale legs. Twisting and turning over the edge of the grass, seemingly oblivious to the world, she raised one arm at a time, her pointer aimed at the sky. In the deepest part of the pool, she stopped, treaded water and faced me.

"Have yuh ever met Annette Kellerman – You know, the girl from Abbie's school?"

I nodded. "Yeah, I did once but I've seen her plenty of times walkin' down Como Parade with Abbie towards Cooblanna – The only time I met her she gave me the biggest fright."

"How's that, Loon?" Horty asked, splashing water towards me and swimming closer. "Tell me."

"It's not a great story, but I was down near the Baths one day, when I saw somethin' floatin' in the water, a little way out. It had stripes on it so I thought it might a' been a drowned sailor. The odd one does come ashore." Horty sat back on the rock ledge beside me.

"Sounds a bit creepy, Loon – I heard their bodies blow up an' their skin falls off."

"Well, I didn't see any skin fallin' off, so I stripped down to my shorts and started paddlin' towards it, which was silly 'cause the water was choppy an' freezin'.'"

"It was Annette wasn't it?" Horty jumped in.

"Don't ruin me story," I replied, shaking my head.

"So, I swam closer, an' I was about to touch it when the striped body rolled over, and Annette's big green eyes opened wide and stared at me – I tell yuh, I nearly pooped me pants! It was like she'd been sleepin' out there ... In her own time she smiled and said.

'Don't be concerned, young fella, I was just practicing holding my breath before I go on to Mordialloc.' "

"Annette's such an amazin' swimmer, isn't she Loon?" Horty said somewhat in awe, "I've heard she's about to put displays on in the city – And yuh know, she taught her entire class how to swim before the end of the year. She just pushed 'em off the diving board at the Baths, an' told 'em to strike out on their own."

Horty was in the process of picking her soaked singlet away from her blotching blue and pink skin, when a girl's voice rang out from near the old path that skirted the surrounding cliff; a thin line of melaleuca and tea-tree along its fringe hiding the pool from all but the most persistent eyes.

*Entre chien et loup un feu s'élèvera*
*Pour bannir les ténèbres et le brouillard méprisés*
*Qui abrite des falaises et mort soudaine*
*Et tromper la lune et la beau marée*

The girl projected her voice, not towards us, but outwards, for only the bay to hear. The words however did manage to echo around the enclosure of the rock pool as we searched for the girl who remained hidden at the top of the cliff.

"No, *beau*'s masculine – It's *belle marée* – bloody French!" The girl yelled in frustration.

"What's she jabberin' on about, Loon?" Horty whispered as she quietly slipped back into the pool.

"The bloody French, Hort," I whispered back, "She doesn't like 'em, just like my dad."

First appearing as a flash of pink and white on the cliff's edge, I caught sight of the girl, a large blue bonnet obscuring her face. She called out again.

"Come here you naughty, naughty dog."

A small fluffy dog, a Pomeranian, with its leash trailing

behind slid under a twisted and bent low tea-tree branch and then ran down what was not a path, but a slippery gully worn through soft dark mud left by the heavy recent rains; a gully which then snaked and descended sharply in the direction of the rock pool where Horty and I kept a cautious silence.

When the dog reached the pool, its lower half covered in mud, it completely ignored us and began to drink the water, only yards from where I sat completely still.

*Go away you little shit!*

"You'll be sorry when I get you, you bad dog." The girl from the promenade called again, this time louder and angrier.

"Go on mutt, shoo!" Horty said in a whisper.

Climbing over the same tea-tree branch as her dog had gone under, the girl appeared in a full-length white dress with a wide pink sash. Slipping from side to side as she tried to negotiate the gully, one hand holding her blue bonnet steady over her blonde curls, the other holding firmly onto an exposed tree root, she managed to creep gradually down the gully's edge.

"Why should *I* always have to walk the dumb dog?" The girl said carrying on an argument with herself and then shouted down at the dog without noticing Horty or me. "You mischievous so and so."

This girl under no circumstance was going to make it down, catch her dog, and then climb back up with it in one arm without covering her pristine white dress and pink sash in mud or at least losing her large blue bonnet.

"Wait!" I yelled up to her. Horty immediately gritted her teeth, shook her head and swam to the far end of the sea grass.

"I'll grab your dog."

The girl froze on the spot and looked around until she saw me shuffling along the ledge to where her dog with its tail wagging had walked into the water; its wet, muddy hair floating on the surface until finally submerging itself up to its head.

"What did you say?" The girl snapped.

"I said I'll grab your dog and bring it up to you. You won't make it back up again carryin' a soaked dog."

"That's what *you* think," The girl, a year or so older than Horty or me stated.

"Who are you to tell me what I can and cannot do?"

*Snooty bloody thing!*

"Suit yaself then." I shouted in reply, not believing her aloofness. I pushed her dog away from me. "Well, come and get it then."

Not a second later and while attempting only one more step, the girl slipped onto her back and slid two yards down the gully; rich soil pooling at the base of her dress which began to concertina onto itself. The girl sat up immobile breathing heavily and on the verge of tears.

"If you still want me to bring up your dog. Just lettin' yuh know I only have my shorts on."

The girl whose cheeks were now glowing red replied while trying to leave herself a semblance of dignity.

"I'll try not to look." She then forced a smile while commencing to scoop black sticky mud away from her backside. Belatedly she added, "Thank you."

I held tightly onto my soaked shorts while I stood, fearing they may slip down, however the girl appeared only interested in her bedraggled blonde curls which had escaped to all sides of her bonnet. I easily picked up her dog as it had waited eagerly for me to exit the pool and then looked over at Horty who still held a disapproving look on her face, shaking her head again to let me know that she didn't want anything to do with this undertaking. It then struck me that reaching the top of the climb with a wet and shaking dog in hand would be no simple matter for me either.

At the beginning, I managed to find and grip onto various rocks and vegetation on the way and made good progress up the steep part of the gully, more than a trickle of water oozing from its sides. I was only yards from the uninterested girl when I fortuitously found a thick tree root to grab onto and was in the middle of making a final effort to reach her when she asked smartly.

"Why *were* you swimming in such scant clothing with so many respectable families in the vicinity?"

I stopped and rested my elbows on the spot, not believing what I had just heard. This girl needed a piece of someone's mind.

"Yuh know, I sort o' like yuh dog – but *you*..." I stated clearly not trying to hide the disappointment I was feeling.

The girl then lowered her head, and a torrent of tears began to flow.

'I'm sorry. It's just...' The last few words disappearing within her blubbering.

With that, I bit my tongue and found the strength to hurry and get this job done. Gripping the tree root tightly I moved myself to within a yard of the girl, able to see tears still flowing freely down her cheeks. I then realized I may have been too hard on her and felt I needed to make amends.

"What's your name?"

The girl looked up and studied my face to see if I was making fun of her. She eventually replied quietly, "Felicity." and shortly afterwards added with a newfound eagerness.

"My folks rented a cottage at the back of Ricketts Point and a bathing box on this side of it, so my brother and I can spend some time at the beach," Felicity then closed her eyes, "Mum told me to change my clothes before I walked down here. I can't go back looking like this."

Another distraction was needed.

"What's your dog's name?" I asked as it wriggled in my left hand, now wanting to get back to its owner.

"Master Brown." She said clearly and with unexpected pride. Instantly from below in the pool we could both hear a giggle, and I had to remind myself, that, of course, Horty was still there. Felicity then looked at me with a strange grin upon her face and asked.

"Is there a girl down there with you?"

"A friend's down there and she's on her own."

"Well … you'd better not keep your *friend* waiting," Felicity stated, speaking as if she was sure there was something more than friendship between Horty and me.

Not wanting to prolong this exchange, as my torso was cold with mud and my shorts creeping down, I managed to pass Master Brown up to a girl finally grateful to have him back.

Once back over the tea-tree, Felicity stood and as she did Master Brown decided it was a good time to shake himself free of water and sloppy mud and leave a final humiliating splatter over her face and clothes. Felicity initially looked like she was about to cry again but held it in and instead forced a smile onto her face. She then laughed and hugged her quivering dog close to her chest.

"Well, thank you again…" Felicity subtly inquired.

"Alistair," I got in quickly.

"Well, thank you, Alistair, for returning my naughty dog, but you'd better get back to your *friend* and have a good wash yourself, which I shall also give Master Brown and myself when we get back at our cabin." Felicity said with genuine appreciation and then gave me a tiny wave as she began to move in the direction of Ricketts Point, her dog straining at its leash, her free hand holding wet dress away from her legs.

After three or four steps, Felicity stopped and spun around to face me.

"Why don't you and your *friend* drop in to say hello to my family at our bathing box," A smile then appeared on her face. "It's the light blue and white striped one in the first row after Table Rock – make it soon if you can. It might stop my parents growling at me."

As Felicity walked away, I shouted in return. "Sure, we'll pay a visit – Can't see why not!"

Halfway down the muddy gully on my way back to the hidden pool, I finally realized why Miss Hortense Brown may have though it funny that Felicity's dog was named Master Brown.

⟡

# CHAPTER THIRTEEN

# Innocence

"**Not sure this is** a good idea, Loon," Horty whinged, deliberately dawdling behind me trying to hold things up, even though we wandered through a quite pleasant she-oak and banksia shaded path that ran behind the bathing boxes and the expansive beach at the start of the Ricketts Point strip.

"I do want to see what this girl Felicity looks like, but maybe we shouldn't be too eager. Only a strange person would be silly enough to go down a gully in her best clothes, chasin' after a dog she didn't want to walk in the first place … and don't forget – her folks might be peculiar too!"

I had had to put up with Horty's grumbling as soon as I suggested we should leave our makeshift camp after our clothes dried and I put the rest of my clothes back on, but now her whining was beginning to grate. I spun around.

"Hort, the fish weren't bitin', so there was no use stayin' at the camp … An' Perce and Sniffle couldn't care less if we left for a while or not." I stated in no uncertain terms, "We were invited so we should at least turn up to say a quick hello ... Who knows, her folks might have laid out cakes and biscuits for us."

Horty crossed her arms and huffed loudly then pushed past me towards the bathing boxes.

"...an' I did sort of promise."

—•—

Horty suddenly put an arm up in front of my face which made me pull up mid-stride. She then aimed her pointer and whispered.

"Look between the huts over there, Loon. Is that the girl you can't wait to see?"

I followed the direction of Horty's arm and saw a girl who may have been Felicity facing away from us towards the shoreline. This girl was in a narrow strip of sand between the two middle bathing boxes out of a short row of four nestled just to the south-east of Ricketts Point; a dog, most likely Master Brown, lay spent and tied on a short lead to the verandah post of the vertically striped hut on the left.

"Gotta be her!" I whispered in return, "The hut's got the right colours."

"Whadayuh think she's up to?"

"Dunno, Hort."

I wanted to end the mystery and call out to make sure it was Felicity, but Horty put a finger up to her lips and whispered through a smile.

"I wanna see what she's up to first."

—•—

Against my wishes we found a comfortable sandy hollow to watch Felicity from, well concealed by bushes in a dune above the huts and beach. Beyond the bathing boxes, a boy of about eight years was building a sandcastle with multiple towers only yards from where tiny ripples lapped the shore.

In a plain summer dress, a contrast to her earlier flamboyant attire, Felicity pressed the back of her sunhat covered head, her elbows, and the palms of both hands against the peeling weatherboards of her bathing box; one foot nervously tapping the plinth board.

Seconds later, Felicity with cheeks flushed, pushed off the weatherboard, turned around and kicked the plinth board with intent. Horty and I smirked at each other unsure of what this unusual display was about. Felicity then appeared to stare at the actions of the young boy as he upended and tapped the bottom of his small tin bucket adding another tower to the impressive castle.

The boy, thoroughly absorbed in every detail, stepped back to study his creation, nodded his head as if recognizing that something else was needed and then ran swiftly into the scrub not far to our right. We lowered our heads but were still able to see the young lad pick up long leaves and gumnuts and then return to spread them across the towers.

"Hugh – Hey, Hughie!" Felicity yelled in a restrained but persistent manner. "Come here."

"No!" The boy yelled back without restraint, losing concentration, and dropping leaves onto the sand.

"I have a treat for you."

"I don't *wanna* treat!" He shouted back, but this time turned around and looked between the boxes to gauge if there was indeed a treat at play.

From inside the blue and white bathing box, a muffled yet cranky voice of an older woman, immediately interrupted.

"Felicity, just thank your lucky stars your father wasn't here when you returned from your mud bath. Don't go making things worse for yourself by ruining your brother's afternoon tea and making me send you back to the cabin."

Felicity fell back against the boards and then slapped them hard with her right hand, then her left. Diving into a deep pocket she rummaged about until finally pulling out a round multi-coloured lollipop on a stick. She waved it in the direction of Hugh who feigned disinterest.

Unexpectedly, Hugh picked up his bucket, gave a dismissive wave to Felicity and then dragged his feet through the sand in the direction of Table Rock, soon to be lost from view. Felicity stood contemplating the lollipop and was in the process of returning it to her pocket, when Hugh suddenly appeared from around the back of the boxes and poked his head into the gap between.

"Give it to me." he said rudely.

"Shush!" Felicity whispered. "I will, but you have to do something for me first." She then waved the lollipop in front of his face.

"What?"

"Come behind the hut. It'll be nice."

"I'm gonna scream yuh pinchin' me, if yuh don't give me the lollipop, right away – Mum'll take the strap to yuh for sure, this time."

Felicity placed the lollipop in Hugh's hand, and then dragged him by the arm around to the back of the bathing box. She then moved her face within inches of his.

"Close your eyes, shut your mouth and don't move."

Hugh blinked but only pretended to be closing his eyes as Felicity pushed her summer hat upwards and then leant down and pressed her lips firmly against her brother's closed mouth. Hugh tried to pull back sharply, punching his sister's arms and body, but Felicity held him in position to make sure she finished the kiss she started. When she finally released Hugh, he spat at the ground, wiped his hand across his mouth, and then punched Felicity as he ran off, lollipop in hand, once again in the direction of Table Rock.

Beside me, Horty had rolled onto her side, holding her stomach as if in pain and kicking me repeatedly in the side; trying to say something but unable to, finally getting out.

"Oh, my Lord! – Oh, my Lord! That's the funniest thing

I've ever seen in my life, Loon – She's pretendin' tuh be kissin' her new beau."

Felicity looked over in our direction and appeared shocked and embarrassed on hearing those words. Horty then cupped her hands around her mouth and shouted.

"Alistair Lundy!" I quickly put my hand over Horty's mouth and whispered.

"Shush up, will yuh. She cries at the drop of a hat."

I felt bad when I looked over to see Felicity facing the wall of her bathing box, crying while touching her lips as if reliving the kiss. Seconds later she ran from between the bathing boxes in the direction of Ricketts Point.

"See what yuh done now," I grumbled not understanding Horty's nastiness. "She's cleared off for good."

Horty stepped in front of me and shook her head.

"Yuh like her Loon!" Horty said confidently before brushing sand from her dress.

"Do not..."

"Yuh do – a girl knows," She said smugly, "Don't worry 'bout what she did then. Lots of girls go silly 'round her age ... Hope I don't."

I took a deep breath in exasperation.

*I hope you don't either, Hort*

—•—

# CHAPTER FOURTEEN

# Dover Slopes

**WITH HEAVY EYES AND** while sitting beside Perce, Sniffle, and I on the shell grit and sand beach at our isolated camp next to Table Rock, Horty said in a tired voice.

"I reckon, I'm gonna head home now."

Three heads turned and looked sideways at Horty to gauge if she was serious about leaving or simply having a lend of us. As she kept staring straight ahead with a determined look on her face it meant that she clearly wasn't. This wasn't a complete surprise as it was well into the afternoon of a full day that had started to feel long for me as well.

"Well, I'm not," Perce shot back, "cause I just caught a couple of pinkies, an' I reckon the tide's about to turn any minute – So I'm stayin' put to get a bagful."

Horty pursed her lips and with purpose grabbed her satchel and threw it over her shoulder while stating. "Well, I'm goin' anyway!"

I was in a bind, part of me was keen to throw in a line and help Perce and Sniffle catch a 'bagful', but other parts of my weary body, mainly my sore chin and my rumbling stomach, wouldn't mind calling it a day.

At that moment ripples began disturbing the surface of the bay giving notice of the change. Both Perce and Sniffle looked towards their lines in anticipation that they would soon be running out into the bay with a large fish on the hook.

Horty no longer caring about fish or tide stomped away from our sand and grit beach to find a path that would take her up through a wall of undergrowth to the esplanade road where she could then follow it home. Seconds later, Perce's line ran out into the bay, and he took off in haste over the slippery rock shelf to secure the catch, uncaring if Horty departed or not.

I threw my satchel over a shoulder and took off after Horty, before stopping only a few steps later and taking it off again. Sniffle stood staring at me with an incredulous look on his face.

"Whadayuh doin Loon?" Sniffle asked in a whisper on seeing my hesitation.

"I ain't caught a fish on my own today, Sniff!"

"Well, it's too late now 'cause yuh can't let Horty walk home on her own – her dad will tan all our behinds if someone doesn't do it – an' anyway, Perce and I've been watchin' the lines here for hours – so we get first dibs!"

After another bout of hesitation Sniffle had had enough of my indecision and pointed in Horty's direction.

"Get bloody goin' Loon!"

By the time I had caught up to Horty she was passing the Great Southern Hotel, where only a handful of visitors remained strolling around its forecourt. Further on under the pine tree where Mrs Toy had sold her wares, all that remained were wispy puffs of steam escaping from the cast iron cauldron and a scattering of empty periwinkle shells.

On the corner of Charman and Beach Road, Horty slid her scratched and dusty satchel from her shoulders and placed it on the grass verge on the high side of the corner; the old satchel no longer the 'feather' she said it would be to lug around at the start of the day.

Before I was to reach Horty, I stopped in the centre of an empty Charman Road to take in the calm waters of Beaumaris Bay before me and the vastness of Port Philip Bay beyond; neatly framed by sheer rock cliffs on the right and high clay slopes cut with ragged gullies on the left.

On the low side of Beach Road, an easel and canvas stood alone at roughly the centre of these two divides; a lady, a tall redhead in a loose green smock stood with paintbrush at the vertical in one hand and a multi-coloured palette in the other, while balancing precariously upon a small hillock offset to the right of the easel.

"Wait on a minute," I shouted to Horty, "I wanna see what she's doin!"

Before Horty could reply the lady called out in a

cultured voice, "She ... is the cat's mother," not bothering to turn around to face us or remove her paintbrush from the perpendicular.

"And *I* certainly am not!"

Horty let out a tiny chuckle and then we grinned at each other at the funny way the lady had replied with a statement that made little sense to us anyway.

"So glad you're amused." The lady huffed just before she made her way unsteadily down the soiled white clay to the base of the rise. "So, unless you are interested in the art of painting. I will bid you farewell."

Horty, who had grudgingly returned her satchel onto her back, joined me in the centre of Charman Road, pushed up her nose and whispered, "La-di-da-di-dah. Lady Muck's not the only person who knows about painting."

I was bemused by Horty's statement, but before I had time to think on it, a small jinker driven by Delvine, the eldest daughter of the Wells family from Beaumaris, came down Charman Road and crossed our path. We said a quick hello and Horty asked if she could again pass on her thanks to her mum and dad for delivering her to near home from St Augustine's on Sunday past. After Delvine had parted down Beach Road for Mordialloc, we crossed over to the beginning of the 'Slopes' and the lady who seemed oblivious to our approach.

Horty and I quietly found ourselves a spot behind the lady and watched as she made multiple dabs and strokes using a thick greenish-brown paint mixture onto a small canvas, and then gently smoothed and curved rough edges away with her pinkie finger. Horty again took off her satchel and plonked it by her side.

"Be quiet!" The lady complained and then held her breath and turned towards the small rise she had just returned from, her smock swimming over her meagre frame. She contemplated it and then resumed painting.

Horty rolled her eyes and pursed her lips but said nothing. We moved to either side of the canvas to view it in its entirety, to simply see if it was of sufficient interest to warrant any further viewing. I expected the lady who was quite tall with a distinctive hunch on her back to be replicating the scene in front of us, but the image of the slopes and the cliffs appeared quite blurred and dull in nature; the beach almost non-existent and the bay swollen out of proportion.

"My dad's new wife used to pose for Mr Conder," Horty stated clearly and properly.

"Sometimes in the nude."

The lady, and I, spun around immediately to look at her. We both studied Horty's face to see if she were about to break into laughter, or in my case to see if there was a deft sign that she was trying to pull a swifty on the lady painter, but her face continued to give away nothing.

"Where?" The lady asked.

"At the East Melbourne studios of the Artisan Painters."

The lady turned her head slightly and took a step closer towards Horty.

"What was her maiden name?"

"Lizbeth Montague."

The lady nodded in acknowledgement.

"I have heard that Conder dabbled in portraiture, on occasion, and I have read he has had some success recently in Europe combining similar studies."

"He painted her twice before he went overseas, and she said he was always a perfect gentleman during her sittings." Horty paused and gave me a sideways glance before continuing, "My new mum..." Suggesting she was coming to terms with her father's choice. "...said Mr Conder had the good nature of putting his subjects at ease while he worked."

"I have been told that is true, and I can see that in the relaxed nature of the subjects in his local pieces – Now, seeing you have an appreciation for the fine arts. What do you think of 'The Slopes at Mentone'?" The Lady asked Horty, and then stepped back from the canvas to leave her a clear view, completely ignoring me, which was fine as I was still contemplating Lizbeth draped in a veil while being painted by a group of lustful men, in a dimly lit studio near the city.

Horty took two steps back, tilted her head from side to side and then nodded.

"I like the brownish colour of the slopes and the cliffs do look – imposing."

*Imposing! Where'd yuh get that rubbish from, Hort?*

She then added, "Sorry, but I have to say the bay doesn't look right. Looks too big. It's not that size at all."

Horty turned her body towards the bay which in the last few minutes had taken on a deeper, more striking aqua-blue colour as shadows began to extend over Beaumaris Bay. A scene much more appealing than the lady's painting in its current state.

"You know. I often wonder how the Heidelberg School could have missed this location." The Lady stated while studying the near vicinity. "They painted from Ricketts Point to Mordialloc and completely overlooked this amazing spot." The Lady's eyes were now beaming with enthusiasm as she discussed her favoured subject, a complete change from her earlier prickly and aloof self.

Horty who seemed to have rallied from tiredness and want for home, searched my eyes to see what I thought of this lady and her surprising fervour for this place.

"Go on," The Lady declared, "Climb to the top of the rise, both of you – You'll see what I mean."

The top of the hillock was the highest point in an area which spanned the lower junction of Charman Road and Beach Road. It had a clear view between the ancient rock cliffs and the decaying clay slopes that stretched eastward into Mentone proper. Horty and I used crude footmarks chipped into clay that threatened to crumble and give way at any moment to climb up and onto the small plateau at the top.

Within seconds of focusing my eyes on the bay, its waters appeared to rise and swell, holding my attention as they grew large and menacing. Colours across the slopes and on the cliffs sharpened with intensity and then just as quickly blurred to the greenish brown painted on the lady's canvas. Horty grabbed onto the sleeve of my shirt, her breath shallow as energy seemed to drain from her body which had commenced to sway from side to side. She closed her eyes and pressed her pallid face into my shoulder.

I swung around afraid Horty may fall and gripped the back of her shirt to stop her from collapsing. Fortunately, she soon found the strength to remain standing and steady her movements. Seconds later with washed-out eyes and a slight embarrassment she looked up to me and said.

"Loon, I'd better go home now. I don't feel well."

I placed an arm firmly around Horty's waist and helped her to the bottom of the rise. The lady was waiting for us and took Horty from me and sat her down gently beside the easel. She then asked for me to step away while they spoke.

The lady rubbed Horty's back and they spoke in whispers while she raised Horty's knees and lowered her head. Minutes passed slowly until Horty sat up and nodded her head to indicate she was feeling better. Once Horty had sufficiently displayed her steadiness of foot, the lady approached me with purpose and stopped with her face close to mine.

"Take Hortense home by the most direct route young man, and do not leave her side." The lady then gained my full attention with her pale green eyes.

"She will be fine."

Before the lady returned to her easel, I thanked her for showing me her incredible painting and the not so innocuous hillock that inspired it. I then went over to Horty who gave me a grateful smile and asked if I could carry her satchel. She then gently touched my arm and pointed in the direction of home.

—•—

# Part Two

# Dorothy – Star from the North

**EARLY FEBRUARY 1905**

**FROM CHARMAN ROAD TO** the bottom of Plummer Road, Horty kept her eyes either down or straight ahead. She strode along at a steady pace and maintained an uncomfortable silence between us. Although no longer appearing tired, she was also just as unwilling to engage. I tried to make conversation by describing the scene I had witnessed on top of the hillock, and how large and unusual the bay looked from up there, as well as how much of a coincidence it was that the lady painter knew Lizbeth, but still no response was forthcoming.

"Did yuh catch the lady's name, Hort?"

"Shush, will yuh Loon?" Horty said quietly, her eyes fixed on Beach Road gravel. "I'm concentratin'."

"On what?"

"Just shut yuh gob, will yuh?"

I got the message and shut my mouth, feeling terrible

that we were unable to laugh about this day and its weird and wonderful, funny and confusing, as well as exhilarating and tiring incidents. Not to mention surviving a solid dust-up with Loz and Roscoe.

After we had turned into Plummer Road, I noticed, even at a distance and in fading light, a horse and rider doing tight circles in front of a group of three well-dressed people at the bottom of the drive at La Plage. The animated scene was enough to make Horty look up briefly from her concentration on the rough track to see a girl of about fourteen dressed in a bright green riding jacket, sitting bare-back astride a coal-black horse, which I presumed to be Devil.

*What the hell is she doin'! – Hope she knows how flighty Devil is?*

When Horty and I were within a hundred yards of the drive, the girl raised her gilt-edged green riding hat, and on her command, made Devil rear up and hold that position, its front legs kicking out in mid-air, while the girl's bare feet dug deeply into the colt's flank. The girl then lowered her hat and the mount in turn. A round of applause went up from Mr Brown, Lizbeth, Principal Miss Ellie Sampson, and even a belated roll of claps from Lucia on the front porch, which gave a certain confirmation that the bold rider was the Browns new boarder from Wodonga, arriving in Mentone well before her expected date of midway through the first term.

"Looks like yuh new boarder's arrived early." I declared

but Horty also ignored this comment and returned to studying the ruts in Plummer Road. The first person to spot us was Mr Brown, who, a touch concerned over the uncertain nature of Devil, changed focus and held both hands out towards the horse in case it made any erratic moves, but this was proven unnecessary as the young lady now standing steadily on the horse's back clapped her hands, dropped sharply onto Devil's girth, and then slid down his side landing effortlessly on both feet. Another small round of applause went up.

"You are certainly a wonderful rider, Dorothy," Mr Brown said momentarily forgetting about Horty and my arrival, his gaze not leaving the confident demeanour of his new boarder. A tap on his shoulder from Mrs Brown reminded him of our approach towards the welcoming smiles of all others in attendance.

"Now, I have a couple of important people I would like you to meet, Dorothy, and I suspect you will get to know them quite well at La Plage." Mr Brown said only short of gushing.

"Come and say hello to our daughter, Hortense, and our good friend and neighbour, Alistair."

Upon reaching the waiting group, I found myself before Dorothy and too eagerly stuck out my hand for her to shake. She extended her hand but just before it met mine, pulled it away and placed her black gloved fingers as a table under her chin, her long and curled eyelashes blinking above large hazel eyes as she contemplated with a grin if she should accept my offer. Seconds later, she thrust her hand forward, gripped mine firmly and then shook it vigorously.

While this was happening and to everyone's surprise, Horty had veered away from the group and was heading up the drive towards the house without a word of explanation. Lizbeth, Miss Sampson, and Mr Brown stood in shock, mouths agape, regarding her lowered head and increased pace not to the front door but towards the entrance to the stables and the rear of the house.

"Hortense!" Lizbeth called sternly, "Dorothy would love to meet you."

Lizbeth could then be heard apologizing quietly to Miss Sampson and Dorothy.

"Young lady! – Can you come and say hello, please? You are being quite rude to Principal Sampson and Dorothy," Mr Brown shouted to Horty as she was about to round the brush fenced entrance to the stabling yard, but she ignored his call and disappeared behind it. Mr Brown then stormed after her. I had to do something to stop Horty from getting a good tanning from her father, so I shouted the first thing that came to mind.

"Horty's bustin' for the loo, Mr Brown – You know she can't talk when she's bustin'."

Lizbeth glared at me knowing that wasn't the case but held her tongue as she must have felt it might ease the over-all situation. Dorothy, however, was still holding my hand and giving scant regard to Horty's departure. She gave a firm squeeze of my hand and the makings of a smile formed at the side of her lips.

"Pleasure to meet you ... Alistair," Dorothy gradually released my hand. "I hope we are going to become the closest of friends."

No sooner had Dorothy walked away to more congratulations from Mrs Brown and Miss Sampson and I had given up trying to figure out what was ailing Horty, than I noticed two figures shuffling up Plummer Road towards us. It didn't take long to recognize who they were. It was Perce and Sniffle both wearing broad grins and looking as proud as Punch as they waved vigorously with one hand, while struggling to hold up with the other, a long stick that flexed close to the ground due to a large brace of fish of various species and sizes strung along its length.

I waved back and then strode off to greet them with an incredible story of my own that might come close to matching theirs.

⬤

# CHAPTER TWO

# The Calm Before...

⁓⁓

## MID-FEBRUARY 1905

I LEANT BACK AGAINST the verandah post, closed my eyes, and allowed the Friday afternoon sun to soak into my skin. I was alone on the side porch at home enjoying a rare occasion during the last week when no-one was making demands on me. I knew Mr Rennie's chief carter would be making demands on me tomorrow morning when I began learning the local bread delivery round, something which should have occupied my mind, but instead my thoughts kept racing back to last Saturday, and the girl, Felicity, who Horty and I had crossed paths with while swimming near Table Rock. I kept wondering how strong the need within her must have been to make her kiss her brother. Horty had made fun of her for being foolish, but I had a nagging suspicion that that same force was powerful enough to make fools out of all of us.

Our house paddock and stabling yard appeared different to me today as I panned around its grassless interior while removing my tight and worn boots. Mum said she would be down in the lower paddock near the banksias clearing a fire break between her hives and tinder dry bracken and I knew Millie would still be at work tidying up after a busy day at Taylors. I suspected that Dad wouldn't be around the house today – and I believed I knew why. I pulled off my boots and began searching for a nail that may be breaking through the sole, when a voice called out.

"Wot wen' on at school, Loon?"

With surprising eagerness for a person who normally couldn't care less for the silly jibes and tattle tales of an ordinary school week, Horty jumped clear of the top rail of the stable fence, uplifting a layer of dust in the yard as she landed. She was obviously feeling much better than she did last Saturday when a malady gripped her which rendered her silent to all and sundry. I turned my boot upside down and the smallest of stones dropped out from the heel of my boot onto the cracked wood of the porch. Horty sat down beside me with attitude and a broad smile on her face.

"Not much," I eventually replied.

I thought twice before deciding against telling Horty about what Mum had let slip this morning on what had occurred yesterday when Dad paid a visit to Mr Rennie's establishment. The story although relayed second hand from a lady buying candles, had Jock putting Dad squarely on his backside with a few well-chosen words after he had stormed into the bakery during the morning peak to demand a more substantial situation and a guaranteed term for my employment, and although I can never be certain of the actual words – what was recounted – rang true.

'If I was Reg and had to look at your almighty scowl each day – I'd leave toon, as well!'

"Oh, forgot," I said turning to face Horty, "Perce got the strap for makin' Rene Marshall cry."

"Wha'd he do – tug her piggies?" Horty said with her legs swinging over the edge of the porch, "Rene is such a sook." Then added.

"…'fore I forget, good luck tomorra on yuh bread round."

"Thanks Hort. Should be right. Mr Hall always seems cheery enough when I see him goin' past."

Horty then looked away and delayed her words,

"An'… did yuh leave a bunch of flowers on the back porch the other day?" She then stopped swinging her legs and stared at me. "Was a goodun' – it had gum, an' wattle, an' banksia, all wound together to make a basket, an' even had a flower made from feathers."

I couldn't be bothered working out who had time to do all that, so I returned. "Nuh!"

I then asked about something I couldn't quite figure out. "You're actin' a bit strange the other day, Hort. You alright?"

Horty appeared disheartened by my comment and lowered her head.

"Jus' felt a bit dizzy that's all. Nothin' for a boy tuh worry about."

The last comment grated on me as girls had the annoying habit of mentioning things and then shortly afterwards telling boys to pay no mind. This was soon forgotten as Horty, and I decided to wander down and pay Mum a visit in the lower paddock. On the way, I asked out of curiosity how her new housemate Dorothy was settling in.

Horty then immediately grabbed the sleeve of my shirt and pulled me up. Mum stood up from her raking and looked over at us, wondering why we had made such an abrupt stop on our way to visit her.

"Promise not to say anything Loon, and never repeat a word of this – Promise?" I hesitated as to what this brash behaviour may be about. Nevertheless, I crossed a finger over my chest and confirmed by whispering, "Cross my heart and hope to die."

"She's a funny one, Loon." Horty whispered and then looked around again. "She *don't* like wearin' clothes."

I gave a quizzical look at Horty, then produced a grin. "Neither does Perce and Sniffle."

"Not funny... From the first day, Dorothy's been *so* loud and wanders about the house with just a loose cord tied around her dressin' gown. She barges into my room and starts singin' and dancin' like she's in a play or somethin' – and bounces high on my bed." Horty then came close to my ear and whispered just above silence.

"And I can see her sometimes."

I pulled back from Horty in astonishment and a little

in confusion as to what she could actually see of Dorothy, and how that would matter anyway – after all, Horty was a girl herself. I thought that perhaps I shouldn't but asked anyway.

"What does yuh dad think of that?"

"He gawks at her all the time, an' I don' wanna know what he's thinkin'. It's so embarrassin'."

"Lizbeth wouldn't mind," I said light heartedly, "She'd be used tuh people wanderin' around in the altogether waitin' to be painted."

"Should never have told yuh about that, Loon, an' yuh better keep stumm about it too – or else." Horty produced a fist in front of my face which wasn't accompanied with a smile.

"Lizbeth has a blank look on her face all the time. I don't think she knows what to do. She can't send Dorothy packin' back to Miss Sampson, just 'cause she's wearin' a loose dressin' gown. That would bring disgrace on the family ... not that I'd care – I'd be rid of her."

"I don't think either of 'em are gonna do anythin'."

When we reached Mum, she made a gesture out of the ordinary and gave Horty a quick hug and asked her quietly how she had been. Horty nodded and said it had been no fuss. We stayed on for a while to help Mum drag the last of the dry bracken into a pile for Dad to burn on a much cooler day.

*I wonder if Mum made the flower basket for Horty.*

—•—

# CHAPTER THREE

## Given the Rounds

MID-FEBRUARY 1905

MR RENNIE HAD TOLD me to be on time, albeit no later than when the sun comes up and go directly to the stables that belonged to his bakery which were situated at only a short distance further down the lane from where I had first spoken to him. Mr Geoffrey Hall, the chief carter was to show me the ropes on how to do the local bread delivery round. I knew this would involve connecting one of two draught horses to its burden and then loading the still warm loaves, buns, and pastries into the cart in the reverse order of removal, as well as placing an odd assortment on the side shelf for people who walked up.

Mr Hall was tall and gangly with a bullet-shaped balding head, which made him as well-recognizable as he was well-received around the thoroughfares of Mentone, where he was always ready to chit-chat with locals as he made his rounds. Customers could expect a cheeky grin and a 'still nice an' 'ot' at their front gate or a loud wrap on the bread tin to let the household know their delivery was safely inside. He even occasionally allowed us kids to ride up front with him on the cart.

"Let's go!" Mr Hall shouted at me the second I stepped inside the entrance to the stable, disturbing the early morning silence and creating a swirl in the dust that floated within. I propped and remained out of his way while he checked the draught horse's reins and trace lines, only allowing myself a brief glance sideways to see if I needed to load any baked goods into the back of the cart. I could smell and feel the warmth of fresh bread, so I had to assume the deliveries were already on board.

"Whadayuh lookin' at?" Mr Hall said stopping briefly in front of me, then blathered to himself as he slammed the rear doors of the bread cart shut. "I don't need this today."

"Let's go!"

I climbed up and barely had time to settle onto the short wooden bench beside him, when we turned right into the small lane and then shortly afterwards left into an eerily quiet Florence Street.

"I'll tell yuh which gates to cart to, I'll do the others," Mr Hall shouted through foggy breath while we bumped and rolled towards Milan Street and away from the just rising Saturday morning sun. "Clopper knows where to go, so don't touch the reins."

"Sayin' that, yuh'll need tuh keep yuh bloody wits about

yuh." Mr Hall said with no attempt to add a 'welcome to...'

I sat quietly beside him and rubbed my eyes clear of a few small tears that couldn't be held back and dared not look at him sideways.

*Did he hate Reg – Is that what this is all about?*

⬥

We turned south into Milan Street and back into more familiar territory. I knew all the half dozen families who lived in this isolated pocket of town, so it gave me a chance for a good start.

"You take the Dowlings and Watts and I'll go to Taunton," Mr Hall grumbled loud enough to wake the whole neighbourhood, "...an' don't be stoppin' to kill no bloody snake at the Dowlings this time."

Mr Hall's packing of the racks in the wagon appeared rushed and haphazard, even to an amateur like me, but I knew the Watts had a large family of six who had a liking for bleached white bread, and before them on the right side of the road was the elderly Mrs Dowling and her doddering fusspot brother, Frank, who only preferred pumpernickel. As I returned to the cart after delivering two loaves to the Watts, I noticed Mr Hall just outside the brush gate of the magnificent ivy-covered Taunton Manor talking to a lady with a tilly lamp unnecessarily in hand and a faded pink dressing gown wrapped close across her chest to ward off the morning chill.

This lady who I knew to be Mrs Hislop, the housekeeper at Taunton and a friend of her equal at La Plage, Lucia, then dug deep into her dressing gown pocket and pulled out a stuffed white envelope and passed it to Mr Hall. I lost sight of what occurred next as Clopper veered sharply right into the recently levelled street that joined onto Plummer Road, dipping as it caught the edge of a freshly dug gutter. Mr Hall joined me as the draught horse showed fresh enthusiasm as it took us directly towards Horty's home.

"I'll get this." Mr Hall said in a more reasonable tone as we turned right to pass La Plage. Again, to my surprise, Lucia was also waiting with an envelope in hand at the end of the drive. Mr Hall strode towards her with two round loaves which he promptly placed in a basket on the ground. Seconds later he took the envelope and made scribbles in a notepad. Lucia then whispered something that I was unable make out.

*I thought most accounts were paid at the shop ... Horty will know what's goin' on*

After making a drop at the Gilberts, on the corner of Balcombe Road, we headed further away from the populated centre of Mentone and through the light fog and solitude of the market gardens before Charman Road. At the end of that long stretch was Sniffle's home set back thirty yards from both roads and I was glad when Mr Hall said I could deliver their crusty loaf. I figured the more time away from Mr Hall and his incessant grumbling would be a welcome bonus.

I got the biggest shock when I stepped quietly onto the Schaufelle's uneven and creaking porch, to look up and see Sniffle standing in the open frame of the front door with only his drawers on.

"Hell, Sniff! – You 'specially like scarin' me?"

Sniffle took a step back into his house.

"Sorry Loon, did'n' 'ave time to chuck more clobber on – How's it goin?"

"Not too good, Mr Hall's a bit of a grump – Here take this, I don't wanna fall behind." I shoved the warm loaf into Sniffle's shivering arms and then ran off whispering.

"Thanks for gettin' up."

⊷•⊶

There were fewer drops north of Balcombe Road with most locals preferring Rose's Cheltenham Bakery. One notable exception was a friend of Mr Rennie who lived along La Trobe Street. Principal Meagher's home already crowded with students receiving extra tuition, and the sun barely up.

I was soon getting the gist of the timing required to drop off the deliveries and then return to the bread cart to reload my arms. I even received the odd friendly wave and a 'Hello! – You're not Geoffrey,' from a man walking briskly in the direction of the railway line. However, every home Mr Hall carted to had someone at the front gate with an envelope in hand. At one house I could clearly hear the owner say, '...can't decide.'

At Perce's home, situated a short distance north of the station in Mentone, I placed three loaves into a metal trunk that had been used for years for food deliveries and had to smile to myself as I listened to the yelling and swearing inside, only just louder than the stomping up and down stairs and careering along corridors.

As we came up to Blackwood's Blacksmith on Balcombe Road, farriers appeared in groups from within the red forge glow of the smoke-filled entrance and began milling outside, the greater part with tongs and hammers still in hand. Mr Hall was soon over with them, shaking each of their hands. The farriers produced envelopes as well as notes and coins from within leather aprons, which they thrust at Mr Hall. Again, I could hear the words, 'can't decide.'

Clopper however, continued casually on his way and headed south down Moorabbin Road and I became anxious when the blacksmith's shop was out of sight. Suddenly, Mr Hall appeared beside the cart.

"I got business to do back at Dempsey's training track, so do the presbytery on the corner, they get two. The other homes 'round Barkly and Childers way, get one. Catch me up at the track on Balcombe."

I nodded thinking this would be all right until it dawned on me that I wouldn't be able to match the deliveries to the houses.

"But I don't know the numbers after the presbytery." I

yelled back to Mr Hall who had already gone a fair way up Moorabbin Road.

"Stop whingin' and just get it done!" Shouted Mr Hall, and with that he was gone, and I was left to do the impossible.

*Is he setting me up for a fall?*

After dropping two loaves into a tin under the oddly shaped roof of the presbytery, I began to panic for what to do next as the draught horse and I headed slowly up Como Parade. I couldn't predict which street Clopper was going to turn into next and it didn't matter that it was Barkly, because by that stage my panic had turned to anger, and I felt as wild towards Mr Hall as I had towards anyone in my life.

*Was he one of the reasons why Reg had walked out?*

I was not going to deliver any bread until I met up with Mr Hall at Dempsey's training track and then hoped to convince him to turn Clopper around and cover the same ground again, but I knew this was foolish and wishful at best, and my career as a bread carter would be over by the end of this round.

Shortly after heading up Barkly Street, I noticed an elderly woman on the corner of Stawell Street, a disbelieving look on her face and a fat envelope in hand.

"Where's Geoffrey?" she yelled at me as she stepped out onto the street, obviously not too happy the chief carter wasn't on board, a wire gate then slammed shut behind her.

"I'm meeting up with him at Dempsey's," I said but didn't

want to complain to this lady about my desperate situation – However, I had to do something, so I jumped quickly off the cart to grab whatever loaf she required.

"I wonder if you could help me?" I asked as steadfast as I could, "Do you know who gets what bread 'round here – it's my first day?"

Keeping up with the cart, the elderly lady who had greying curly hair, wiped down her flour-stained apron, rolled her sleeves up over blotched and sagging arms and then told me to leave her round loaf inside the gate. I had seen this lady around town before, but didn't know her name, neither which explained the envelope. In a deft move for a large lady, she lifted herself up and onto the wooden bench seat staying close by the edge, for a time the wagon rocked from side to side until I climbed back onboard.

"I know who gets what around here ... and not just bread," She said with unflinching certainty, "and I know what Geoffrey's going to get, too."

I had to let Clopper follow his well-tried route even if it meant going around blocks whose deliveries could have been covered in one sweep, which also included heading down Como Parade twice until we straightened again along Barkly Street to head towards Dempsey's training track.

At the back of a small crowd that had gathered to watch a single horse parade in front of them, albeit a large chestnut and a muscular one at that, was Mr Hall. When he turned to see the elderly lady sitting on the bench beside me, his eyes almost popped out of his head. Leaving the crowd behind, he raced to where Clopper and his first-time passengers were turning left into Balcombe Road.

"Mrs Wright – truly sorry," Mr Hall apologized in a cloying manner, "I honestly forgot you wanted to be involved, but I see my young charge has brought us together while there's still time."

Mrs Wright, her expression still none too happy, stepped down awkwardly from the cart and passed her envelope to Mr Hall who then took up her position.

"Well, I'm holding you to what we talked about on Thursday morning, Geoffrey." The housekeeper's chest heaving as she kept up with the cart.

"My word is my bond, Mrs Wright."

"Well, it better be – and I'll tell you another thing, Geoffrey. You're going to get yourself all undone, not just with your punting shenanigans but with letting a young lad do the round for you on his first day."

With that, Mr Hall sat upright and nodded in acknowledgement of his dressing down.

"This is an absolute once off, Mrs Wright, and it certainly won't happen again." Mr Hall returned as nice as pie, before shifting closer to me and showing his gritted teeth.

Mr Hall now in a hurry did the bulk of the deliveries south of the railway line, not only trying to make up for lost time but I'd like to think for his rotten behaviour on what was meant to be a training day. As we finally turned back into Florence Street and I could see an end to my time with Mr Hall, for today at least, he dug into his heavy pockets and produced a shiny coin. He then forced the coin, which was a new shilling, into my surprised hand.

"Now, keep yuh bloody mouth shut about t'day Lundy," Mr Hall quietly sneered, "or your next round will be shittier than yuh first."

❖

As if nothing had happened, Mr Hall and I swept out the cart and returned Clopper to his stable, bathed and brushed down for another day. I went to leave via the bakery lane at the same time as Mr Rennie entered the stable. "Allo laddie," he said cheerfully before searching out his chief carter. Outside the stable, I could just make out Mr Hall's reply to Jock's question on how I went today.

"As good as yuh can expect for a lad still wet behind the ears."

❖

My dad, who had been displaying a more cheerful manner since Mr Rennie put him in his place at the bakery, came in for dinner after a long day, saying that while in the lower paddock a passing rider had sprouted about a fortuitous occurrence in Mentone.

"Apparently, half the town put their money on a local horse called, Can't Decide, who romped it in in the main race today and they all made a pretty penny on it."

Mum was incredulous on hearing this.

"Why didn't anybody tell *us* about it" She said plonking a pan down hard onto the cast iron stove top, "We can always do with a few more quid in the kitty."

I kept my mouth firmly shut.

⬥•⬥

# CHAPTER FOUR

# Something's Afoot

### Mid-February 1905

ON THE FOLLOWING MONDAY morning, Dorothy entered the sorority of the Mentone Girls' School at Cooblanna House. On Tuesday afternoon, Valentine's Day, Abbie Taylor paid a surprise visit to La Plage and asked Lizbeth and Mr Brown if she could talk privately to Horty about her future, with the expectation that there would be a bias towards her joining Dorothy at her new school.

Horty hadn't spoken to Abbie since the chance encounter with her tram at the beginning of our fishing trip, this time Abbie was in a no-nonsense mood. Lucia prepared afternoon tea for Abbie and Horty in the back garden.

— • —

Horty couldn't wait to tell me about what happened the next morning when she caught me off guard on our way to school. Rapid footsteps alerted me of her approach only seconds before she jumped on my back when we were half-way across Weatherall Road.

"Guess who came around yesterday, Loon." Horty then snatched the woollen cap off my head, took off hers and tried mine on at an angle. "Yuh cap's so comfortable," She worked it closer onto her head. "Can I have it?"

"No!" I replied sharply, closing my eyes and wincing as my back continued to ache from the amount of lifting and climbing from the cart during Saturday's bread round.

"Who's a grumpy bum t'day?"

I went quiet for a time not wanting to make obvious my discomfort and continuing disappointment about what had happened with Mr Geoffrey Hall, but I couldn't help myself. "Dunno if I'm gonna stick with the bakery. Wasn't much fun."

Horty rubbed her eyes and said as if bawling. "Wasn't much fun, Mr Jock," and then in a horrific Scottish accent, "Boo-hoo, laddie – Get back on yoor caaart!"

I didn't know why but Horty having my hat was making me cross, however that wasn't what was making me angry. I had to shake off my grumpiness.

"Who came around yesterday?" I asked. Horty was at once engaged.

"Abbie! Bit curious she turned up at home without warnin'. She already knows I don't wanna go to her school. I told her that on the tram, but I said I'd listen."

Horty waited until we were close to the gates of Cheltenham State School before she continued.

"She ignored me in front of Dad an' Lizbeth, an' didn't speak to me until after Lucia had left tea for us in the garden. Then she winked an' leant forward to say,

'Something's afoot.'

My eyes were open at that, I tell yuh, but Abbie shushed me up an' shook her head. Before I knew it, she was speaking so loudly about how Principal Sampson was such a wonderful teacher, an' how her sisters and mum were as good. She kept saying things like 'The Follity Club needs you.' 'They need a property warden.' blah, blah, blah. In between, she whispered. 'Lucia came into our store on Saturday, looking for anything new for around the house. All innocent, she started telling me about how your parents had made big plans – for you!' ... all innocent, for a big fat blabber mouth."

*For God's sake, go to Cooblanna, gotta be betta than walkin' all the way up here ev'ry day*

At the school gate Horty handed me back my cap.

"Lucia said to Abbie that my dad and Lizbeth's minds were made up. 'Maybe it'll work out better if Hortense doesn't go to Cooblanna.' Lucia overheard 'em sayin' 'She could take up a position in the firm as soon as the end of the first term.' Bet Lizbeth can't wait to get out of Mentone and start strollin' down Collins Street with her painter friends. Lucky, Abbie put me straight on what I gotta do.

'Don't ever work for your family, Horty,' she said,

'everything changes. Dad makes me do all the rotten jobs he doesn't want to do. Fortunately, Millie said early on she would only work in the store. I've got to go and collect the rent from our tenants, most of whom are good, like the Chinese, but there are plenty who pretend not to be home or say they are waiting on money.' "

I was happy to go through into the school and not have to hear any more of Horty or Abbie's family babble, but Horty stood fast in front of the gate.

"I hate goin' out to our holding yard at Dingley, Loon. The men are so dirty and are always complainin' about their pay an' equipment – An' don't forget – in the off-times, I'd have to mind Samuel, or entertain Dorothy."

Horty was complaining more than me earlier, and I was about to make fun of her with a better Scottish accent, when she continued her bluster.

"Abbie then told me somethin' interestin'. She leant back and said loudly.

'I won't be asking you again, Hortense.' and then whispered, 'Members of the Follity Club get to leave class early in the afternoon and go and help Annette get in and out of her mermaid costume in the city and often stay on and watch her perform. Sometimes we go over to Collins Street and stare at all the fancy people.' Abbie gave me a big smile.

'So, instead of being stuck at home working for your family – You'll be free to go into the city with me and the Follity girls!' "

Horty stepped to the side of the gate.

"Loon – I got no choice."

---

"I'm gonna rip off the scab." Horty could be heard saying just above the screeching and shrill excitement of children happy to be leaving the disciplined confines of school for another day. Sniffle and I were only a step behind her when she pushed through the squeaky school gate of Cheltenham State School number eighty-four, hoping that while we were walking home, she might add to the astonishing tale that La Plage's housekeeper Lucia had gossiped to Abbie Taylor.

I had told Sniffle and Perce about Horty's dilemma as we lined up for class in the morning, however the only response I got from a half-interested Perce was, 'She ought a' go where she's told to...' Sniffle was more concerned thinking neither choice was fair and that she 'should be able to stay with us.'

Horty caught us off guard when she turned left onto the footpath and continued to walk towards the railway line instead of turning right to take our usual route south into Mentone. Sniffle and I stepped off the path and looked confused at each other.

Horty yelled back to us, "I'm gonna wait for Abbie to get back from Mentone an' tell her I wanna go to Cooblanna.

So, don't neither of yuh put in yuh two bob's worth an' try an' stop me."

Seconds later, Sniffle shouted up the path.

"What rot are yuh talkin'? Yuh shouldn't listen tuh any old drivel that gets spread 'round town!"

Horty, utterly determined about her choice, paid no attention to Sniffle's claim, and kept walking towards Taylor's Realty and Auctions.

I kept my mouth shut because it wouldn't have made any difference what I said, Horty wasn't going to change her mind, because it *was* the right thing to do – Get in before someone else decides your life. And as far as not seeing Horty around that wasn't going to happen, our homes were only a couple of stone throws apart – and besides that – in Mentone, you can't avoid running into people you know, even if you try.

⬤

# CHAPTER FIVE

# *Great Excitement*

## Late February 1905

"Tu-dah!" Millie sprang into the living room, placed a bright yellow frock with wide puffed sleeves over her light blue work skirt, and a beaming smile on her face. In astonishment, I looked up from studying a detailed illustration of Little Lord Fauntleroy in the Argus, and thinking of how closely it resembled the lad we saw in a sailor suit at Ricketts Point. At the same time, Dad glanced up from his favourite seat near the window, his pipe soon drooping from his open mouth. By the sideboard, Mum stopped pouring a small dram of honey mead and took the dress in with bulging eyes.

"What do you think?" Millie directing her question principally to Mum. She then swung herself and the dress around in a tight circle.

"It's wonderful, Millie." Mum declared, placing the bottle of mead carefully back onto the sideboard and then taking one dram over to Dad, who to Mum and my surprise had requested it earlier in the afternoon.

"I know you had it in your mind to buy a dress for the welcoming do Abbie's school is putting on for Horty and her new boarder, even though I said I would help you make one from any pattern you chose – but it's done now."

"No Mum, it's not like that. I never expected to be able to afford one. Abbie was in the city on Saturday on the lookout for bright material to make dresses for the show, when she came across this shop in the backstreets that sold dresses rich women used to own and at a fraction of retail."

"I like it!" Dad threw in, making everyone turn and stare at him, unaccustomed to hearing him comment on any female matters.

"Thanks Dad, I hope it's not too garish for local tastes."

Mum had another look at the dress from top to bottom. "No, not at all." Mum assured, but I suspected without total honesty. I had to be straighter down the line.

"Yuh wanna have a good look at yaself in the mirror with it on, Mill, 'fore yuh go wanderin' about town – People might think a giant canary is on the loose."

Millie held her breath and glared at me, her anger rising. For my part, I had to stop myself from bursting out in laughter, thinking I had said something clever. Suddenly, Millie's back went up, and her eyes burnt into mine.

"How would *you* know *anything* about what people should wear – Have you had a good look at *yourself* in the mirror lately? – You look like a steamin' dag off a sheep's bum!"

Mum took the dress off Millie and felt its material, but Millie wasn't finished with me yet.

"Don't know how you're going to get *any* girl to dance with you at Horty and Dorothy's welcoming do," Millie fired and straight between my eyes. Her words took me aback, not particularly by what they were suggesting, because we could basically say anything to each other and no offence would be taken, but by the fact that I had never thought about how I appeared to other people.

*Can't be that bad – Can it?*

—•—

Halfway down the hall with my night candle in hand, Dad called out to me from the back verandah saying he wanted a word. At first a dread ran through me as I remembered our previous talks and how they had dispirited me for days. As Dad's moods had been more pleasant lately and he hadn't called me outside for a while, I followed without opposition and even with a small amount of intrigue.

I put down my candle on top of the pillar at the side of the verandah ready to sit down on the porch when Dad called me further into the mottled darkness near the wood-shed. When I found him, he took a deep breath and turned his eyes upwards, studying the streaky white clouds that flew low overhead.

"They're different to us..." Dad whispered to the sky as if trying to convince someone, perhaps God. I stared at the distraction in his eyes; confusion tilted my head.

"Women... Girls, I mean," Dad continued, his eyes lowering to look straight at mine.

*The girls I know ain't that different ... Women might be*

I nodded in vague acceptance, yet still none the wiser as to where our talk was heading, as Mum had taken me aside two years ago and with love and in detail told me about the birds and bees, so that couldn't be it. Dad could see my attention was wavering, so he changed his tone to a cheerier one and even patted me on the shoulder.

"Alistair, what I want to say is, you and your mates will get together and talk about girls and how you'd like to kiss them and such and that's fine. Girls, I'm sure, will do the same, although you're never likely to hear it. However, certain boys, who are nothing more than show-offs and skites will brag all over town about their conquests."

Dad aimed his pointer at my face.

"I *never* want to hear any of that talk coming from your mouth, or a solid clip will be arriving behind your ears – Got that?"

I nodded until Dad knew my acceptance was genuine. He lowered his finger and spoke softly.

"Girls at times will treat you bad. That's the way it is, so you'd better be ready to take it on the chin and let them move on. I know it's difficult at your age, but if you keep one thing in mind it will make things easier." Dad had a quick look back at the house, where only the candle in his and Mum's bedroom was glowing.

"You've got to make a fuss over a girl, make her feel important. If you ask a girl to a dance, compliment her on her hair, her dress, something. They put in a lot more effort than young blokes do. Sure, you will dance with other girls during the evening, but keep an eye out and make sure the girl you took gets lots of dances – and remember to take her home at the end of the evening – She might even give you a kiss at her front door."

Dad's talk was good, but I sort of wished it would end at that.

"Right, we should get back in," Dad said to my unease, "Mum will be wondering where we are." I was ready to move but Dad placed a hand on my shoulder to stop me. He then said slowly and deliberately, the dull light from the low moon showing an anguish on his face.

"Before we go in I want to try and explain something to you."

I had no idea what this change in mood could be about but steeled myself for the worst as I could see Dad's body tense and his gaze fix upon me.

"You probably think I've been hard on you lately, and you probably could argue a case for that, but at your age you don't know enough about life and how it can deal you knocks and hardships out of nowhere." Dad took his hand off my shoulder and I noticed his shoulders sink from an unseen weight.

"The main reason I want you to work at Mr Rennie's bakery is for you to learn the value of money and how hard work delivers it. Your mum and I have had difficulties in the past that have left us with not a single penny to our names – That's a feeling I never want you to experience, ever, because ..." Dad's voice faltered as he tried to control his emotions.

"...having nothing will eat at your insides until you can no longer look at yourself in the mirror – and worse things than that can happen."

Dad had a quick glance back towards Horty's place and I knew by his pained expression what he meant.

"I probably worry too much about how you will go at the bakery, Alistair, which I shouldn't, because as far as I'm aware, Mr Rennie and Mr Hall are fine and honest people and will always do the right thing by you."

*He doesn't know one of them!*

"Yeah, they've both been great and shown me lots of new things," I lied as straight as I could.

"Can't complain at all."

Dad nodded his head and then tapped me on the shoulder. We were walking slowly back towards the house, when he added in a more light-hearted way.

"And Millie is right, you do look like a dag off a sheep's

bum, so get yourself a haircut well before the skating rink do, so you don't look like a freshly shorn sheep ... and another thing, Mum wants you to get a new shirt."

Dad stepped up onto the back porch and stated as a final word.

"Seeing you're earning your own money. You can manage that on your own."

*Haircut – new shirt!*

I didn't even know how much I would be getting paid as a bread carter once a week, most likely a pittance, but it didn't matter, I had just found a whole new respect for my dad.

◆•◆

# CHAPTER SIX

# 'I Smell a Rat'

## EARLY MARCH 1905

THE WAY THINGS STOOD with my new job, it was only a matter of time before Mr Hall sacked me or forced me to leave. The following bread rounds were no better than the first, in fact slightly more humiliating, often having people on corners or even down quiet lanes coming up to the cart to shake Mr Hall's hand and sing his praises for delivering them the much-needed winner in Can't Decide. For the rest of the time, he basically ignored me and gave silence when I asked him how much longer it would be before I was ready to do a round on my own. I couldn't go through every Saturday like this, but on the other hand I couldn't be the second Lundy to walk out on Mr Rennie in a short period of time.

Something had to give.

I asked Sniffle and Perce the next Monday at school, if they knew anything about horse racing. Sniffle said he knew nothing and didn't care for it either. Perce said he and his brothers sometimes went out early in the morning before school and walked the adjoining paddocks between his home near the railway line and the Mentone Racecourse to watch the trackwork take place, for no other reason than it was something to do, and they were usually up early anyway fighting or playing tricks on each other. I asked if he would go with me one morning to the track so I could have a look for myself. He didn't even ask me why.

The next morning well before the sun was up, I made my way past silent houses along Balcombe Road, until turning north into Swanston Street and walking the two blocks up to where I met Perce at the end of his street. He looked as fresh as a daisy, whereas I couldn't stop yawning and wanting to crawl back into bed, even one at his place. We crossed Point Nepean Road currently void of all traffic, before trudging through dewy paddocks on our way to Mentone Racecourse. After almost twisting my ankle while stepping knee deep into a grass choked drain running alongside Moorabbin Road, it occurred to me that this cross-country foray too early in the morning was a fool's idea destined for failure. It smacked of desperation to try to figure out why so many people loved horse racing.

*This is a big mistake!*

Strolling through the open ticket gate, Perce and I

propped ourselves on the high ground beside the grandstand, the sun barely peeking over the fog shrouded farms and market gardens this side of Dingley.

Despite this gloomy scene, a hive of activity was taking place around the track below. Steam poured out of horses' mouths and off their saddle-clothed backs as scarfed trainers and strappers led them here and there, the morning silence only broken by the rhythmic pounding of hooves on the sparse turf as jockeys urged their mounts on by hands and heels close to the running rail. Perce stepped in front of me and then pointed in the direction of the finishing post.

"That's where we gotta be Loon, with the punters and touts." Perce said with confidence and then took off.

*Perce loves horse racin' – that's for certain!*

Men of various standing, with hats pulled low and collars up on their gabardine coats, huddled together to form small groups along and behind the mounting yard rail, talking in whispers as they smoked pipes or toked at roll-your-owns, their heads up when a horse and jockey rounded the bend.

"Watch the fobs come out now, Looney." Perce said with more than a hint of excitement as men left their huddle and lined the fence beside us. Sure enough, fob watches came out as they watched a dappled grey fly into the straight and line up against the rail for its run to the post. Timing began about a hundred yards out and ended as eyes looked down sharply at the second hand as the horse flashed impressively across the line.

"I saw that little filly trial a couple of weeks back at Epsom," An old-timer said in a drawly whisper to his neighbour behind us. Perce elbowed me in the side.

"It burnt off a genuine sprinter that had won at Caulfield – next two starts she finishes stone motherless at Pakenham and Aspendale – I smell a rat, my friend. I think she's set for a plunge and not in cold water."

"Fiddle!" His off sider replied with scepticism. "Some horses fly in the mornin' an' flop in the afternoon."

"Where they takin' the horse for a plunge, if not in cool water?" I whispered to Perce who immediately began shaking his head.

"Bloody Hell, Loon! Don't yuh know anythin' about horse racin'? – Bettin' plunge!" Perce whispered back into my ear, "They keep a good horse under wraps until it gets good odds with the bookies and then – Smack!" He punched his right hand into his left.

"Yuh rollin' in dosh!"

*I'm never gonna pick up this crazy horse racin' jabber*

"D'yuh know this horse?" I asked Perce, thinking this filly might be worth following.

"Her name's Amelie, an' she's bein' trained at Epsom by the Anderson Brothers an' I believe she's runnin' here on Saturday." Perce said pushing me along the rail and away from the older gentlemen, "Whatever yuh do, don't get carried away with all the idle claptrap yuh hear touted 'round a track – Certainties run thicker and faster than yuh mum's honey."

I wasn't completely convinced by Perce's over cautious advice, and I certainly wasn't going to dismiss out of hand what the old timer had said about a plunge. He may be onto something, and I might be able to use it to my advantage.

"We better go Perce, Ol' man Meagher, don't take too kindly to latecomers." I said, edging my way towards the ticket gate.

"Stop bein' such a worry-wart Loon. This is what life's about, not stuck in a stinkin' classroom. Tell yuh what, come with me next Sunday mornin' an' yuh can help Mr Manning and his lads take their horses down to the beach for a swim. Best part is an old lady who lives in Stawell Street comes over and cooks up a great pile of scones for us when we get back."

"Is she a big lady with spongey grey hair?"

"She sure is, Loon – D'yuh know her?"

"Might do..."

—•—

I was almost bursting to talk to Mr Hall about horse racing as soon as I arrived at the bakery stables on Saturday morning. I was beginning to feel it had an excitement about it I never expected. It was out of the ordinary, a welcome break from the day-to-day. In a lot of ways, it wasn't even about the money, although a winner could make life a lot more comfortable. It was about the ultimate challenge: beating the odds, even if occasionally you were left without a zac.

However, it wasn't Mr Geoffrey Hall's voice I heard as I neared the stable; it was Ernie Hudd's from the produce store, walking towards me from the opposite direction.

"G'day, Loon!" He said cheerfully on seeing me, "Pickin' up the routine?" It was a welcome surprise to hear such a warm greeting on my arrival at the stables, although it also meant Ernie had no idea about the other side of Mr Hall's personality.

"Gettin' there, Ernie! – Ten times better than school." I said enthusiastically but without honesty, only to avoid repercussions. At that moment Mr Hall came out through the stable doors, said hello to Ernie and then shook his hand, telling me without a glance to 'get out back and load a good mix of spares this time.' However, every word they spoke echoed clearly back to me as I said hello to Clopper.

"Got any good oil for this arvo, Geoffrey? There's nothin' jumpin' off the guide for me."

"Nothin' jumpin' off for me neither, Ernie." Their voices fading as they moved out of the stables. "Tryin' tuh keep things a little on the hush-hush this meetin' anyway. Don't want old Jock gettin' a sniff."

"Fair enough, just thought you might have another 'Can't Decide' in yuh pocket." I glimpsed Ernie through the stable doors pulling out a pinch of tobacco from a Havelock pouch, loosen a paper from his lips, and then roll a tight cigarette in one hand,

"Did yuh know your young fella Alistair was out at

trackwork on Tuesday mornin' – He might a' heard somethin'?"

During the silence that followed, I could imagine the sceptical look on Mr Hall's face.

"Lundy – Bullshit!"

"Dinkum, my brother Perce was with 'im. Might be worth askin' the question."

My ears were up on hearing this. I couldn't wait to tell them about Amelie.

"Lundy, come 'ere!" Mr Hall called a second later. At the time I was all fingers and thumbs with a load of bread in my arms, which I came close to dropping.

"Almost done."

"Right now!" Geoffrey replied angrily. I dumped the loaves as best as I could in the side of the wagon and then walked out in quick time.

"Yes, Mr Hall." I said politely, on seeing his displeasure.

"You been down the track this week?"

"Yes." I said positively, trying not to blurt everything out in one go.

"Well then, see any nags that are worth mentionin'?"

"Only one, but I don't know if it's a genuine chance," I said, now aware I could be making a donkey of myself by sprouting about things I knew little.

"Well, if you keep it to yourself, you can cart all the bread today," Geoffrey said his bony hands placed on his hips, "Whadayuh think Ernie?"

"We'll decide if its genuine or not, Alistair, so you'd better cough it up."

Ernie, I believed, was trying to do the right thing by me, so I did as he said.

"On Tuesday morning, I saw a young filly called Amelie run a fast time, according to a small group of punters there. An old bloke said to his mate that it ran stone motherless in its last two starts and he could smell a rat."

Ernie and Mr Hall looked at me with scepticism, and then their heads turned to look at each other, while their faces contorted in mistrust. Ernie nodded his head. "That filly has good breeding. She's racin' here on Saturday so she might be worth having a few bob on, just in case."

"I've heard of it, but if I'm gonna to do my dough," Geoffrey said, his expression hardening, "it's only fair that the person who delivered this certainty does too – That's the way the world works, isn't it Ernie?" He nodded his head in agreement.

*Thanks Ernie*

"I have your first pay in my back pocket, Lundy, for the end of the round. So, what I'm gonna do is help you out," Mr Hall had a laugh towards Ernie, who remained unmoved.

"...I'm gonna place it on the nose of your filly, Amelie – and just to be fair, I'll match your bet."

*But I'm not allowed to bet!*

"You in, Ernie?" Mr Hall asked evenly, to which he added another nod.

*No! I'm gonna do my pay for sure! Then how am I gonna pay for a haircut and a new shirt for Horty's welcoming do?*

# CHAPTER SEVEN

# *Vincit Omnia Industria*

**MID-MARCH 1905**

**PRINCIPAL ELLIE SAMPSON HAD** recommended to Lizbeth and Mr Brown that Horty should reside at Cooblanna for the first month of her tenure at Mentone Girls' School. She had assessed her academic levels and deemed them well below her future classmates' standard. Therefore, Miss Sampson devised a concentrated program that would require long hours of study and minimum disruption. Dorothy was to stay at La Plage. Sniffle and I went over on Sunday afternoon to see her off.

A great deal of stomping of feet and raising of girls' voices could be heard through the open front door of Horty's stately home. Sniffle and I leant back on our elbows and stretched our legs over the porch steps onto the white stones of the drive enjoying the quite amusing fuss and banter going on inside. Her senior school colleagues: Abbie Taylor and Lucy Green, and her year above, Dorothy, were in Horty's room helping her prepare for what would be another major change in her life.

"That dress is *far* too short, Miss Brown." The strict order coming from Lucy, followed by a round of giggles. "Young ladies, for modesty's sake! Your hems *must* drop well below your knobbly knees ... are you listening girls?" This time cackling followed.

"Yes, Miss Ellie – No, Miss Ellie – Whatever you say Miss Ellie!" Added Dorothy smartly, followed by stamping on the floor, which would have been her.

"...and don't forget to practice your Latin roots, while you're washing the roots – of your hair!" There was silence before Abbie burst out laughing, a strange thing to hear from a normally staid person. All this hubbub overseen at a distance by Lizbeth, Lucia, and to my surprise, Mum, who Lizbeth had asked over to 'help out' if Horty became 'emotional.'

"This is not a convalescent home, you two." The deep stern voice of Mr Brown caught Sniffle and I off guard as he appeared from out of the stabling yard and strode towards us beside the brush screening,

"If you were one of my boys, I'd give you a toe up the backside."

*If I was one of your boys – I'd move state!*

"I want your lazy bones to bring out whatever the girls

have decided upon, and don't drag anything across the floor. There should be at least one trunk and an assortment of luggage, enough for a voyage to England and back." Mr Brown grumbled and then while walking backwards towards the stables pointed towards the front door. "Have 'em ready by the time I bring the buggy around."

"We should a' stayed home, Loon. Then he'd have tuh do it all himself." Sniffle muttered as he stood and then reluctantly made his way across the porch, eventually poking his head through the front door and yelling. "Sniffle and Loon Cartage Contractors – At your service!"

I dragged myself slowly towards the door, still unsure how I was ever going to explain to Mum and especially Dad how I had lost all my first pay on the races.

—••—

In the dim coolness of the hallway, a large cane trunk had been placed squarely outside the open door to Horty's bedroom, where I could hear Sniffle shuffling about inside. At the end of the hall, cheerful female voices continued their patter from behind the closed door to the kitchen and I could even hear the gurgles of Samuel being passed around.

I stopped on my way to the bedroom to study one painting out of a half dozen hanging in the hall, one that had attracted my attention on the few occasions Lucia had allowed me in this part of the house, Sniffle and I usually relegated smartly to the kitchen or the stables beyond. The painting was a wonderful depiction of sailboats resting on shore below the clay cliffs only five hundred yards from where I stood, the scene drawing me into its tranquil yet powerful setting. It was also a quiet place I used to go to when I had to get away from everyone.

"Whadayuh doin' Loon?" Sniffle's whiney voice shook me out of my daydream.

"Just lookin'…"

Sniffle was standing at the far end of the trunk glaring at me while gripping the handle, his shoulder already bent for the lift, "This is bull," he whispered in annoyance, but then must have remembered who we were doing it for. "Guess Horty'll appreciate it."

*She'll appreciate gettin' away from Dorothy!* I should have replied, but instead leant down, gripped the near handle, and prepared for the weight.

Outside, Mr Brown was standing at the top of the drive holding the bridle of his horse, the tailgate lowered on the buggy, a glower on his face. We struggled across the porch, shaving its polish at times, until we reached the front steps, knowing we were not going to get this hefty trunk down without taking chunks of wood out at each drop. Mr Brown intervened.

"Alistair, go back and grab the rest of the luggage. I'll take your end. Neville and I will take it from here." Sniffle's eyes nearly popped out of his head on hearing those words.

"Go on!" Mr Brown said to my hesitancy, "Get on with it!"

◦•◦

I had never been inside Horty's bedroom in this house or had seen more than a glimpse through the door. I suspected no-one was inside but gave a solid knock on it anyway; something I would never have done when I called on Horty in her old home now dilapidating north of La Plage; things were different when her real mum was alive.

The first thing I noticed was the sweet fragrance of perfume in the air, mixed with the subtle earthiness coming from the local bush just outside the open window. A new leather school satchel added its own distinctive scent as it rested against a suitcase, not as daunting in size as I had been expecting; a tag in a pouch tied to the handle had Tasmania crossed out and H.B. written beside.

Below the window was Horty's bed, as it had been in her old house, this bed however had a thick quilt covering and two plump pillows in comparison to the sheets and a thin bed spread of the former. On the wall beside the bed was a cross-stitched sampler that stated: *Hortense*, on one line and *From God's Garden* on the line below. In the far corner, a full-length dress mirror stood with Horty's straw hat hanging from a shoulder, its golden ribbon drooping below. On the wall opposite the window, the veneer of an

185

ornate wardrobe shone in the late afternoon sun.

The two things I was hoping to see were in clear view on top of the chest of drawers at the end of the room, one, a pile of shells which included a decent shark's tooth from Mrs Toy's secluded inlet, the other, the flower basket that Mum had recently given to Horty. To the right of the basket a diary lay open. Regardless of how angry Mr Brown may become, I had to have a look at the basket, not having known Mum to make anything like it before.

On closer inspection, she had delicately entwined each branch and stem to allow the blooms and hobs to stand out on their own. However, the flower that impressed me most was the one made from feathers, possibly from a kookaburra.

"It's beautiful, isn't it Loon?" Horty startled me from behind. I went to turn but she had already stepped by my side.

"It is..." I replied quietly, glad to catch Horty on her own before she left, "Haven't seen Mum make one like this before."

"She hasn't. She said so earlier." Horty then came close and whispered.

"Listen up Loon." She looked back cautiously at the open door. "Just lettin' yuh know I asked Miss Sampson to send me to Cooblanna, so I could get away from Dorothy, for a while anyway. I can't study with her annoyin' me ev'ry day."

"But you'll be in there for yuh birthday."

"Can't be helped."

I could hear the door to the kitchen opening and female voices becoming clearer. "But you'd better turn up for the skating rink do." Horty said in a rush, "Quick grab the suitcase."

As I turned to get the case, I caught a glimpse of the open diary that was showing today's date. Scrawled by a hand other than Horty's were three words: *Callum loves you.* Horty quickly shut the diary and took it over and shoved it deep inside the new satchel, grabbed her straw hat and then shouted through a smile.

"Go on! – Get on with it!"

◆◦◆

"Mrs Brown, Lucia, and the girls were such good company today." Mum said looking at me sideways as we walked the quiet, shady lane that separated La Plage from our home, "I enjoyed every moment."

"You know, Mrs Brown has lived such an interesting life. She told us how she had to fight every step of the way to attain the position of office manager in a large plumbing supply company. That's where she met Mr Brown ... She even said she used to be a model and had been painted by the likes of Conder and McCubbin."

*Bet she didn't mention she was sometimes in the nuddy!*

"You know, this is going to be a big change for Horty, isn't it Mum?" I stated more in the way of conversation than with any real concern that Horty wouldn't cope. My real concern however was how I was going to explain to my parents how I had gambled away my first pay – without blaming it on Mr Hall.

"Though, I reckon she's in pretty good hands at her new school."

"I think Cooblanna will be the making of her," Mum said confidently, "because I haven't heard a bad word spoken about the Sampson's School," A quiver noticeable in her voice, "I only hear positive things like how they encourage each girl to take every opportunity."

"Believe me, in the greater part of this world – Women are rarely considered beyond child raising."

Mum deserved better than being lied to about my pay. I had to come clean.

"Mum, I gotta tell yuh somethin' – I've been stupid…" I started gingerly, disappointed in how I had even let this happen.

Mum, instead of pulling me up to ask me how, stared straight ahead at something that had caught her attention at home.

"Did Millie mention she would be bringing Mr Hall – and another man around home today?"

I immediately looked up to see Millie standing nervously behind our front gate. My gaze then shifted to the left and Mum's honey shed, where two men were standing and talking, one being Mr Geoffrey Hall, the other a tallish man not recognizable as being from around these parts. The tall-ish man who had severely parted black hair, and too clever a smile, pointed in our direction.

"No Mum. I dunno what Mr Hall's doin' here – and I dunno the other smarmy character."

*There's no chance I'm gonna put up with Mr Hall going out with Millie*

"Remember your manners when we get there, Alistair." Mum touched my shoulder and pointed for me to get the gate. Once open, Millie tried to put a good spin on the scene.

"Hi! ... It's not what it looks."

"Well, it looks like two men are on our property and Dad's not here – Unless you can tell me otherwise." Mum now quite annoyed by this surprise.

"It's just a coincidence. Mr Hall's here to see Alistair. The other man I do know, and he's here to talk to you and Dad about the Mentone Girls' School do."

"You had plenty of opportunity to let me know about his visit this morning."

"Mum," Millie whispered, becoming upset herself, "I wasn't sure he would turn up."

"Righto, why don't we go inside then." Mum said turning sharply towards the house. "Dad should be back any minute from the Glebe Spring."

Mr Hall having left the honey shed said hello to Mum as she strode towards home with Millie and her mystery man trailing behind.

"Lundy – You kept me waiting a good while."

"Sorry, Mr Hall. Didn't know you were coming."

—•◦•—

I walked with Mr Hall back through our gate and into the lane.

"S'pose yuh heard..." He said pulling up directly in front of me.

"Yeah, Perce Hudd told me this morning when we were taking Manning's horses for a swim. He said Amelie put on a good show but no chocolates." I said as friendly as I could muster, sure he was only here to rub salt into the wound.

"She was beaten by a pretty good filly called Pagan Girl, who flashed home and just got her on the line. Yours started to run out of puff about thirty yards out." Mr Hall continued to stare at me.

"I thought that might happen."

*You bastard! You knew all along...*

Mr Hall then pointed sternly at me. "Listen, you're not a bad lad, but don't think you can go out one morning to the track and think you know about punting. It ain't that easy. You've got to study the breeding, know the trainer, know the jockey, and know what the horse does every time it steps out onto the turf."

"That's why I backed Pagan Girl ... It'd been set for the race."

*I'm a bloody fool!*

"And another thing, just because I show up here doesn't mean I'm after your sister – I saw the look you gave me." Geoffrey's angriness giving way to a smirk, "I do have a chat with Millie when I see her walking along Balcombe Road. However, I have a lady-friend of my own. So there's no need for the dark looks."

"I didn't think..." I started but Mr Hall cut me short and again pointed a bony finger at me. "Yes, you did."

There was nowhere to hide from it. "I did..." I replied quietly, knowing my time with Mr Hall would soon be ending. Mr Hall nodded his acceptance of my apology.

"My lady-friend lives with her family on a small holding between Mentone and Mordialloc. We talk about getting a place of our own near there to put a string of horses on. The blocks are too pricey 'round here."

Mr Hall had a quick glance towards La Plage.

"We still need to get a good deposit together though. That's why I take a risk with the punting, because carting pays rubbish, and most people don't even consider it a job fit for a man."

*Can't he just get it over with and give me the chop?*

"And soon I'll be losing my Saturday round, where I get most of my commissions for doing a community service by placing bets for locals who follow my tips and can't get to the track themselves."

"It wasn't my idea to take anyone's job – I never even..."

I cut myself short, not wanting to be a coward by placing the blame on Dad. I could have stood up and taken the consequences.

"Anyway, Jock's taken the decision out of our hands. You'll be on your own in a month." Mr Hall then started rummaging through his pocket.

"I put your pay on Pagan Girl at five to one. You can work out the return." Geoffrey shoved a stuffed envelope into my hand.

"Don't try and be someone you're not Alistair. People see through that."

Mr Hall then strode off along the track leaving a low cloud of dust in his wake.

—•—

# CHAPTER EIGHT

# Skating Rink Hall

ᥫᩣ

## LATE MARCH 1905

ON THE VAST HARDWOOD dancefloor, a dozen couples swirled in a freestyle waltz to the new and rollicking piano melody, The Entertainer, performed by the always in-demand local sextet, The Music Masters. On one side of the hall, a large group of boys stood in a tight circle shouting and cajoling each other while looking tentatively over at a line-up of girls seated along a row of benches that ran the length of the opposing wall. The boys tugged at the high and stiff collars of their bleached white shirts, while contemplating which girl they would like to dance with.

The 'wallflowers' on the benches, in bright floral dresses and white gloves, continued to preen themselves but could do no more than wait patiently until the boys gained sufficient courage or interest to come over and relieve them of their boredom.

One person I did keep an eye on was the tall man with

the smarmy smile that had come around home two weeks ago to ask my parents if he could accompany Millie to this event. He had failed to impress at the time, yet here he was dancing and holding my sister too tightly in her canary yellow dress on the 'girls' side of the hall.

After a signal from Abbie Taylor off-stage, the leader and piano player of the band turned and gave a nod to his fellow musicians to take the coda to the final bars of The Entertainer. With that, excitement spread rapidly throughout the crowd, firstly as cheeky hand claps or churlish guffaws among the mass of young lads, including Sniffle, Perce, and I, who moved out of our protective circle closer to the stage to witness for ourselves the revealing spectacular that had been rumoured.

With the background sound of props being moved and the odd raised voice behind the curtains, the older attendees made a slow and polite shuffle from the rear of the hall closer to the new boards of the stage. The wallflowers were the last to move and after sitting patiently for too long, stood and surged forward from the left of stage in a restrained jostle.

A further wait only increased the anticipation, until finally a barely recognizable Principal Miss Ellie Sampson, stepped between the curtains at centre stage in the black capped uniform of a stationmaster. The crowd greeted her with a warm round of applause, making her wait patiently for the clapping to subside and silence to return to the crowd, before she could begin to swing a glowing red lantern from side to side.

"And now, Ladies and Gentlemen, boys and girls, the Mentone Girls' School's Follity Club is proud to present one of their favourite melodies tonight, performed not only by their own amazing artists but featuring two welcome additions to their number, and decidedly to our school – One well known to everyone here – Miss Hortense Brown!"

Instantly, a loud round of clapping and cheering went up.

"...the other, recently arrived from the fair city of Wodonga – Miss Dorothy Briggs! ... Please give them and all the girls a warm welcome!"

Another round of clapping and cheering resounded throughout the crowd as assistants drew back the curtains to reveal a station platform with a prominent Mentone sign dominating centre stage.

"All aboard!" Miss Sampson hollered as she exited stage right at the same time as The Music Masters, broke into the popular tune Bill Bailey. Some boisterous whistles were then directed at Dorothy as she raced onto centre stage in a short frilly dress as Mrs Bailey. She then stretched out her fishnet covered leg and placed a high-heeled and pointed shoe on top of a leather suitcase, which sent a small gasp throughout the older section of the crowd. She then looked around angrily, kicked the suitcase over and commenced to dance and skip to all corners of the stage in search of her husband.

Lucy Green, an experienced stage performer then appeared as a male porter pushing a baggage trolley across stage. Dorothy aimed a finger at her and sung.

*Mister Baggage Master, you seen my Bill?*

Lucy shook her head and then hurried her trolley off stage. From the opposite side, Horty skipped on confidently, swinging a suitcase carefree.

*Hey, Miss Passenger, you seen my Bill?*

Horty also shook her head but then commenced to waltz the suitcase off stage like a dance partner. I searched throughout the crowd and found Mum standing beside Lizbeth, and Dad next to Mr Brown, all close to the front of the stage, clapping proudly. A welcome sight I never expected to see in my lifetime.

*Engineer, Fireman, and Brakeman, too,*
*My Bill ain't come home, tell me what to do.*

A huge round of applause went up when Mips Kellerman as Bill Bailey and a natural performer like her sister and brother, slid onto stage in shiny spats, white teeth gleaming from her black painted face, hat and cane in hand like a negro minstrel. Mr and Mrs Bailey then began to tap dance in unison while singing the chorus.

*Won't you come home Bill Bailey*
*Won't you come home*
*I moaned the whole night long*
*I'll do the cookin' baby, I'll pay the rent*
*Lord knows I've done you wrong*

Mips then tap danced around Dorothy as a chorus line of six Follity girls marched and twirled batons behind them at centre stage.

*Remember that rainy evenin' I drove you out*
*With nothin' but a fine-tooth comb*
*I know I'm to blame, well ain't that a shame*
*Bill Bailey won't you please come home*

Dorothy shouted. "Get outta that card game!"

*Bill Bailey won't you please come home*

Dorothy and Mips with raised arms and wiggling fingers then sung the final chorus together, the crowd joining in to build the song to a rousing finale.

*...Bill Bailey won't you please come home...!*

—•—

A group of boys at the front of the hall stepped aside to let Horty through after she had finished talking to our parents outside an internal stage door, these same lads continued to gawk at her like they had never seen her before as she strode towards me, even though she had thrashed them at knucklebones only a month earlier. Horty with her stage make-up still on stopped in front of me.

"Great performance, Hort!" I said clearly making sure she took in every word.

"Thanks Loon – My feet are killin' me though."

"Happy birthday for Thursday, too." I said finding it hard to believe she was the same girl who had pressed her face into a flyscreen two months ago and said to Sniffle and me, 'I ain't goin!' to Cooblanna.

"Ta Loon." Horty returned and then waved over the crowd to a group of girls I didn't know.

"Did the girls do anythin' for yuh birthday?"

"Yeah, the senior girls were great, they made toffee for all the classes, who sang Happy Birthday to me ... it was nice – Dorothy, of course had to show off and ended up with toffee all through her hair." Horty smiled and then looked suspiciously behind.

"What's wrong with those clods?"

"Dunno, prob'ly never seen yuh with lipstick on – They'll get used to it."

Horty gave a quick shake of her head as if she wasn't sure that would be the case and then looked around the hall as the band struck up a marching beat to the Soldiers' Field.

"Talkin' about Dorothy," Horty shouted louder than the music and directly into my ear.

"Haven't seen her since she got changed?"

I screwed up my face, turned sharply and caught the roll of Horty's heavily made-up eyes, which said to me, she couldn't care less where she was, but she had to, because while helping move her luggage from La Plage, I had over-heard her dad and Lizbeth give strict instructions that on this night, Horty was to make sure Dorothy was intro-duced to as many locals as possible and to *not* leave her out of things.

"Nuh, haven't seen her since Bill Bailey." I replied, my sentiments along the same line.

*A small amount of Dorothy will do*

Horty then stared past me towards the open entry doors of the hall.

"She might a' gone outside tuh get some fresh air. It's as hot as Hades in here." But there was doubt in her words.

"Perce and Sniffle ain't come back from havin' a pee, either." I added, and the penny was ready to drop.

The dancefloor by now was crowded and only a handful of wallflowers sat and waited patiently for the ever-decreasing circle of boys on our side of the hall to ask them to dance.

"Bert, Cec, and Big Luke are missin' too," Horty said through pursed lips, "Bet Perce's showin' Dorothy his favourite game."

With that Horty gave a sharp stamp on the hardwood floor and then strode towards the exit. I followed and could almost see steam coming out of her ears.

Turning right after exiting the skating rink hall, Horty marched at a rapid pace towards the perimeter of the building, until pulling up sharply where a couple of palings from the wooden fence of the adjoining property, jutted out dangerously onto the Brindisi Street footpath.

Horty and I poked our heads through the gap in the fence and peered with the aid of dappled light onto soil recently laid and levelled for a new tennis court; the mottled scene only broken at the rear of the property by streetlighting from Mentone Parade. As our eyes adjusted to the lack of brightness, we could also see a further glow emanating from the enclave at the rear of the building; figures nearby creating shadows from within. Horty and I could hear muffled laughter and even a tiny giggle.

"They're at the builder's dunny, for sure." Horty whispered with a fair degree of annoyance in her voice. We then squeezed ourselves between palings and stepped cautiously over the soft powdered sand. Horty took the lead and made straight for the small enclave which we knew the construction company used to store their grading rakes and rollers; it also held a makeshift toilet. Before we entered the enclave, Sniffle stepped out from the gloom and into our path.

"Wait up, Sniff?" I whispered, making him flinch as I almost slammed into him. Without missing a beat or uttering a word, Horty continued around the corner into the enclave.

"What's happenin' 'round there?"

Sniffle was reluctant to stop but replied. "Whadayuh reckon. Perce's playin' 'Don't pee on the seat'?"

"He just beat Big Luke and wants tuh take on anyone who's got any dosh."

"Is Dorothy there?"

"Sure is," Sniffle made a grimace, "Her and Lucy Green are playin' up to the lads like yuh wouldn't believe,"

On the rare occasions that I found myself at Perce's rambling house it was no surprise to find him, and his brothers engaged in a dangerous, hard-fought, and often gross game. The mayhem that ensued as their multitude fought for household supremacy for no tangible prize had to be seen to be believed. This was one of the more questionable games I had agreed to join in. One that I lacked the steadiness of hand to master.

"Don't yuh wanna watch anymore, Sniff?"

"Nah, seen it before – Perce's too good," Sniffle punched me on the shoulder. "See yuh inside."

Sure enough, after I had turned the corner into the enclave, Perce, with a tilly lamp held high in hand, was holding court in front of the open door to the makeshift toilet. Horty had found Dorothy and was standing next to her and Lucy Green, who with both hands over her mouth, kept letting out tiny nervous giggles.

"I'm gonna make it more fair for any lad who'll take me on," Perce declared as he panned his lamp across the dozen or so assembled. "Sorry Big Luke, but you're a poor piddler!"

Restrained laughter went up from a half dozen lads who went over and messed up the abundant black hair of the unabashed Big Luke Marshall.

"Now, c'mon lads. I'm gonna pay thruppence for any lad who can pee straighter than me – for the risk of only one measly penny." More cheers went up from the gathering only making Perce raise his arms and lamp towards the starry sky, exuding an excessive amount of confidence in his own ability.

"Come on, only a mere penny – How 'bout youse two, Bert and Cec Young? You're the best swordfighters in the school toilet block," Perce pointed at the unmoved lads and then leant forward and whispered loud enough for the gathering to hear. "And I hear yuh got plenty o' dough, too."

"Thruppence for a couple o' tinkles and twinkles – That's all!"

There was shaking of heads among the small crowd. Horty looked sideways at me to see if I would step forward.

"I'll do it!" Dorothy called out seconds before silence fell over the crowd and all eyes shifted onto her raised chin and heavily pencilled eyebrows. Lucy let out a shriek while Horty closed her eyes and lowered her head.

"A girl – well that *is* wonderful!" Perce declared with astound, "Dorothy from the Riverina, in fact, has accepted my challenge," He then cupped his free hand and whispered to a couple of lads who stood nearby. "This'll be easy."

Dorothy then stepped forward and did a full bow and even a curtsy in front of everyone.

"I've only got one thing to ask, and I'll pay an extra penny for it – If I lose!" The crowd unaccustomed to a girl with so much front, listened with intent.

"Is that I may give a kiss on each cheek of my opponent for good luck – and if he is a gentleman," Dorothy pointing towards Perce. "Allows me to pee first."

A slow chant of "Do it! Do it! Do it!" commenced and grew to its climax with Dorothy again bowing to the crowd. Horty by now had covered her face with both hands, I suspect in shame.

Dorothy walked up confidently to Perce, leant forward, and then gave him a peck on his left cheek, but instead of moving back, she ran her lips across his and onto the other cheek. Perce wavered in his stance; his eyes wide with the shock of her intimacy before he began to stare blankly into space.

Big Luke handed a porcelain flask full of water to Dorothy who had a large drink, she then handed it to Perce who quaffed his head back and drank the flask dry.

Luke with tilly lamp in hand, held the door open for Dorothy to enter the toilet. She then lifted her dress to expose her bloomer-less smooth and tanned legs before saying with a cheeky grin. "No peeking through the cracks lads, or you'll surely go blind from contemplation."

With that Dorothy nodded to Luke who closed the door, clicked the latch shut and then guarded the door from sneak peeking eyes. Seconds later, we could hear creaks as she stepped up and gained her balance on the wooden seat. Silence again fell over an eager crowd who waited anxiously for the first twinkle.

Eventually it came and it was substantial. Lads shook their heads and whispered to each other, 'She's peed on the seat for sure.' Thirty seconds later Dorothy dribbled to a finish in the smelly tin below.

Dorothy soon after emerged triumphantly from the toilet, a smile from ear to ear and then pointed towards the interior and a dry seat. "See! – Not a spot from Dot."

During the whole commotion I had kept an eye on Perce and noticed his increasing unease. He held his legs together, played with the buttons of his fly and picked through his pants to his drawers.

The boys at the gathering seemed to have confidence that Perce could match Dorothy, as he stepped up and stood legs apart on the toilet seat. Luke got the nod and closed the door leaving Perce in darkness. The crowd listened in anticipation and was kept that way for an inordinate amount of time. Eventually, a wee came as a burst, before it reduced just as fast to a dribble before bursting forth again. Perce could then be heard cursing under his breath.

Taking everyone by surprise was the voice of an elderly

man shouting wildly through the hooped-wire gate set into the wooden fence that separated the unfinished tennis courts from the cricket ground. He cursed as he tried to swiftly unlock and open the gate.

"What the hell are you little buggers doin in there?" The old man then coughed and spluttered, "Wait till I get my bloody hands on yuh!"

Boys and girls took off in all directions until they realized that the only way out was where they came in, through the missing palings in the tennis court fence. A bottleneck of pushing and shoving ensued with the odd kid tripping over in haste onto the Brindisi Street footpath. In all the commotion, Big Luke had forgotten about Perce and had run off lamp in hand to escape. I was in two minds myself but ran over to the toilet just as Perce exited. I grabbed the front of his shirt and dragged him in the direction of the missing palings.

"What took yuh so long in there, Perce?" I yelled as I could hear footsteps thudding after us.

"Somethin' happened, Loon." Perce replied gingerly.

"What somethin'?"

"Somethin' strange..."

"Whadayuh mean strange?"

"Shuddup Loon an' run – I'll tell yuh later."

With that, a shower of gravel sent from the hand of the bellowing old man fell over Perce and my white shirted backs as we threw ourselves in panic at the gap in the wooden palings; slipping through I nicked my arm on a loose nail. Perce and I then tumbled out together onto the footpath. Quickly scrambling to our feet and without daring to turn around and give the elderly man an opportunity to recognize us, we sprinted for our lives towards the entrance to the skating rink hall.

Perce flew up the steps and into the foyer a split second before I made the decision to have a look at the scratch on my arm that had begun to sting furiously. I also wanted to avoid having to stand in a line before the enraged old man. I ran to the opposite end of the skating rink hall and then to the shadows at the rear, from where I could peek around the corner and notice anyone coming.

—••—

With the faint glow from a rear window in the hall, I studied the scrape on my arm and began to dab at the small amount of blood weeping from it with my handkerchief.

"You'll live, Diddums!" A girl's familiar voice declared from within the shadows.

*No! – It can't be.*

But it was Dorothy's voice, and it had to be her standing in the darkness further down the wall. At waist height a small red glow appeared and moved around in a circle. The red glow then moved higher illuminating Dorothy's face as she drew on the cigarette attached to the end of a short holder.

Dorothy lowered the holder and then blew smoke away. "Are you after something Alistair?"

*She's in the biggest trouble if she gets caught smoking*

"No, just keepin' outta the way till the old man goes," I replied through heavy breath, while racking my brain as to how I could get away from her. "He'll go inside and complain, for sure – he would 'ave seen me and Perce."

"Don't worry about the old codger. Lucy says he's a friend of her grandpa and can hardly see a thing." Dorothy stepped closer to me, close enough to see how heavily made-up her face was.

"That peeing game was fun, Alistair. Shame the old fella interrupted us – Still, Perce owes me thruppence."

"He don't like bein' beaten," I added, "...but he will cough it up."

Dorothy took another drag from the holder and then blew smoke towards me, to which I held my breath until the cloud passed.

"Do you like dancing, Alistair?" She then did a short wiggle of her hips.

"Call me Loon, all my mates do." I replied, avoiding the sorry truth that I had two left feet.

"Didn't see a lot of good dancers from backstage." Dorothy said then stepped past me and had a peek around the corner towards Brindisi Street, "Some fine-looking lads, though..."

Dorothy then indicated with her pointer for me to come

closer to her, which I did after hesitation, and before I had time to say no, she had placed the tip of her cigarette holder between my lips; the palm of her hand resting against my cheek.

"Draw in."

I could have resisted, but out of curiosity took a drag from the holder for no other reason than to try something that I had witnessed so many adults do each day and did wonder what the attraction was. Within seconds I pulled back sharply and coughed heartily at the ground.

"Oh, God! – That's terrible."

"I hope he likes girls." Dorothy whispered to herself before removing the spent cigarette from the holder and grinding it into the sandy loam below. Becoming uneasy in her presence, I forced myself to say cheerfully.

"I might go back inside, Dorothy."

Before I could take a step, Dorothy grabbed my arm and turned me sideways into the darkest shadow. She then drew me close to her with strong hands that had moved swiftly around my waist, and kissed me forcefully, her lips all over mine.

I was at a loss for what to do. I had kissed a couple of girls before but never as aggressively as this. I could easily have broken her hold and pushed her away but didn't want her to run off and create an embarrassing scene that could reflect badly on both of us.

Dorothy pushed me against the brickwork of the rink hall,

and then stopped kissing me briefly, her warm breath on my cheek, only to start again, this time in a gentler manner.

"Mind if I cut in?" Horty's voice whispered from close by.

Dorothy pulled back sharply, her concentration broken by this unexpected interruption and by who had caused it.

"Sorry, Hortense," Dorothy apologized profusely, stepping back even further. "Didn't realize I was working your paddock."

"You weren't to know," Horty said in an appeasing way, slipping her body in between her new boarder and myself. "We'd like to keep it mum ... You understand?"

"Yes, sure do! – You can count on me."

Horty then moved her face forward, entwined her fingers within mine and commenced to kiss me so gently and softly that it immediately sent a tingle through my body.

Again, I was unsure what to do or why Horty was doing this or what it meant for friends who were closer than brother and sister. My logic told me to push her away, but my body wanted to draw her closer, close enough so that our entire bodies touched and would never be separated.

Dorothy was suddenly by our side, her smudged red lips close to Horty and my face, her arms draped over our shoulders.

"My! My! You two little kettles are ready to boil. I'd better leave you to it."

Dorothy squeezed our shoulders and then kissed both our foreheads before turning swiftly and leaving. Horty and I made sure she had disappeared around the corner of the skating rink hall, before we could let out a huge sigh of relief. Seconds later Horty stepped back and whispered.

"She is such a scourge, Loon. Don't know how much more of her I can take."

"She certainly is forward," I said quietly, my mind in a complete whirl about what had just happened.

"Sorry I had to do that, but I never seen a girl so ravenous for boys in my whole life." Horty said as she let go of my hands which left me with a deflated feeling.

"If I didn't show her we were serious, she'd never let up on yuh – Believe me, yuh don't wanna be like Bert and Cec Young gawkin' at 'er with their tongues draggin' on the floor."

Horty grinned and punched my arm, while also giving no indication as to how she may have felt about our kiss. Seconds later I was on my own.

I pressed my forehead against the cool brickwork of the rink hall; my heart racing as fast as the city train, my breathing laboured, and my thoughts all in a spin.

—•—

# CHAPTER NINE

# Annette

ඌ ෮ ෨

## EARLY APRIL 1905

**THE ROCKING MOTION OF** the city train had sent me off to sleep, and I fell deeply into it. The heavy and odd shaped parcel that Mips Kellerman insisted I take promptly and personally to her sister was resting securely on my lap and between the tight grip of my hands. In the dream that followed, I saw Annette partially naked, sitting proudly on a wave swept rock in the middle of a raging sea, her long brown hair flowing temptingly over her breasts, the lower portion of her body, the silvery tail of a fish. My dream then drifted to Mentone Beach and a young lady I found floating in the bay, a young lady who may prove to be the closest thing to a real mermaid this country will ever get.

At eye level, Annette's aqua-blue change-room door had only a set of calm waves painted from hinge to door handle.

With one arm holding securely onto the heavy parcel and with the screams of competitors and supporters in the nearby toboggan run in my ears, I knocked on the roughly hewn timber of her hut, inconspicuously tucked away beside the comfort stations at the extremity of the bustling Princes Court entertainment complex. In the dank humidity beneath the massive span of the water chute which dominated the surrounding skyline, I heard a faint shuffle of movement within the hut and shouldn't have knocked again.

"Hold your bloody horses will you – Bloody hell!" A muffled female voice called out in annoyance from behind the door. I took a step back, already nervous, and now possibly on the back foot with the biggest sensation, man, or woman, in this town. The door flew open, and a girl appeared before me, a hand holding closed a white corded dressing gown across her chest. She looked me up and down.

"I know you," The girl said under dark-brown wavy hair, held up and off her forehead by a navy scarf. She then added after a smile, "Whatcha got there?"

"It's a parcel Mips, I mean Marcelle your sister, said you needed for a new performance tonight." I said to the girl who I was sure was Annette, although appearing a lot older than the schoolgirl I had recently seen walking with Abbie Taylor along Como Parade.

"Yes! I have been waiting with bated breath for its arrival.

Thanks for getting it to me so prompt," With a glint in her eyes she looked lovingly at the parcel. "It's a modification I hope will make life a lot more comfortable when I attempt my..."

"Hey!" Annette's words were cut short as a stocky man in a pork-pie hat, pushed his bulldog body and face towards us through the crowd, yelling and grumbling to himself as he swayed from side to side in his rush.

"Is that little bugger givin' you trouble ma'am?" He said in a barely graspable Cockney accent, bowing to Annette as he arrived. "I can give 'im short shift back to where he came from, if that's to yuh likin'?"

"No, that won't be necessary, Alfred. I know this lad and I will show him how to get back to where he came from when we are both good and ready." The minder disappointed that Annette had not allowed him to grab me by the scruff of the neck and turf me out, tipped his lid to Annette and then stepped back to where he had come from, giving me a dirty look on the way.

*Another Geoffrey!*

"I don't know why Mr Baird insists on me having that gorilla outside the door," Annette stated in a whisper as she held open the door for me to carry the parcel into the dimness of her small dressing room. "I can look after myself." Annette left the door ajar and then pointed towards a bed.

"Over there, thanks – Alistair, isn't it?"

"Yeah, that's right." I nodded with relief on realizing that

Annette was a reasonable person. I placed the parcel carefully on what was nothing more than a sagging camp bed and then turned to leave.

"I'd better be off then." I said happy in a way to leave our encounter at that.

"What's all the rush, Alistair? My company isn't that bad – is it?" I held my ground wondering if I should shake or nod my head. Annette came to my aid, "Tell me what you've been doing since you rescued me at the Baths."

I was chuffed that she had remembered that day and I replied cheerfully, "Not much. Started work a month or so back as a bread carter."

"That's nice." Annette said with what may have been feigned interest and then shut the door, obviously feeling safe enough with me. "You're a friend of one of the new girls at Cooblanna – Hortense, I think."

"I am. Hortense says the senior girls like Marcelle and Abbie have been helping her out heaps, giving her lots of confidence. Hortense said if I ever made it in here, I should look out for her near the Pierr – Pierrars." Annette grinned broadly.

"Pierrots – They're sort of seaside clowns – Great fun and incredibly talented."

"She said she'd prob'ly be with the Cooblanna girls."

"I'm a Cooblanna girl, Alistair, don't forget that. I hope they're not leaving me out of things." Annette said with a smirk on her face, although not entirely in jest.

I shook my head not sure how to respond, but instead looked around at what was quite a dingy and stuffy room, with none of the luxurious furnishings I would have expected. Dominating the centre of the room, a concertinaed dresser screen supported a dozen forms of attire flung over its centre panel. Hanging from a hook on the rear wall, a scaled silver and green mermaid costume dripped water into a low bathtub. On a curved metal runner, a bed sheet covered what was likely to have been a toilet and basin.

"At least I have my own loo," Annette answered a question I would never have dared ask and then stepped behind the partition. Seconds later the corded dressing gown flew onto the centre panel to join the other apparel. "I've also met the other new girl, Dorothy – She's a force that one. I'm told she put on quite a stunning show at the skating rink."

"She did – in more ways than one." I replied but then realized I should have kept my response brief.

"She put on another show somewhere else, did she?" Annette asked in a curious tone.

"No..." I replied nervously at being caught out, unable to think of what to say next.

"Sorry Alistair, I'm pulling your leg," Annette threw in from the other side of the screen to ease my anguish, "I heard about the dunny game – She did a remarkable job for a girl."

I could hear coat hangers clinking and scraping as I assumed Annette lifted dresses out for consideration or alternatively shuffled others along a metal rack I could only imagine.

"Going to stay humid, Alistair?" Annette asked, I believed only to confirm, to which I assured 'Pretty sure all evening.' Two arms raised above the screen, but I couldn't make out what form of dress was being slipped on.

Annette then stepped out from behind the screen in a sheer green silk dress, which clung firmly to her body and emphasized her muscular frame and full chest. I continued to stare.

"All girls get them Alistair." I looked away but kept wanting to look back.

"Sorry, I..."

"That's alright Alistair, natural to be curious."

Annette then slipped into flat shoes.

"Feel like a walk? It looks like the Follity girls have abandoned me, although it would be nice to step out with a young man for a change." I nodded in acceptance, ready to leave behind the humid confines of her room. Annette grabbed a short wooden object from on top of her alabaster bedside table and then flicked it down to reveal a fan emblazoned with a dragon symbol.

"Do you like it? One of the geishas left it for me."

*Gayshuz! What are they?*

"You must come and say hello to them in the Japanese Tea House – Such delicate creatures."

Hooked over the last panel of the screen, Annette took

off a green string-tied bag, and then pulled out from within a pair of round spectacles with green lenses that matched their pouch.

"The salty water makes my eyes quite sensitive to light, so I have to wear them, but they do look rather…" Annette posed in front of a blotched round mirror above the bedside table. "Ready?" she asked before pulling back the door to let in blinding light. The first person I noticed as my eyes adjusted was Alfred the minder still standing guard in the shadow of the public change-rooms. Annette called out to him.

"I'm taking this young gentleman for a tour of the park, Alfred. I feel confident he can protect me." A raised hand cut short the minder's reply. He touched the rim of his hat in acknowledgement. Out of range Annette gave me a wink and placed a hand under my arm. "You must try some sencha."

*Sencha! – Gayshu! What's wrong with English?*

Annette led me through a wall of joyous laughter coming from women displaying high and wide floral hats above long white dresses, and the more imperious conversation of dark suited and top hatted men trying to impress these same ladies by pointing out various attractions and watching for the slightest sign of delight.

"This is a most foolish generation, Alistair." Annette stated ignoring the stares and whispers too obvious around us as a thrilled crowd gave us passage.

"The heavy attire women must endure in this heat is appalling, and all because of silly convention. The men are no better, stuffed into dark suit pants and jackets – Melbourne's weather is too fickle for that type of stubbornness."

We stopped to watch the finish of a camel back taboggan race, which in a recent note to home Horty had said she competed in with Lucy Green. In the current race, most spectators were cheering wildly for a largish couple whose male partner while trying to force the toboggan forward to catch a slim couple who dared not move but just hold on tightly to each other, had almost fallen out of the back of the rollicking vehicle. The larger couple managing to pip the lighter on the finishing line, creating an extra load roar.

"The taboggan is by far the best attraction in the park." Annette stated without a hint that she may be downplaying her own show, "So much fun for the competitors, and I have seen several couples go off to the side and have a kiss immediately after a race, win or lose."

Annette gave me another smile before guiding me towards a pavilion that had bamboo screening to all sides and a shingle tile roof above; a sign painted on a panel, read: Japanese Tea House. Annette then stated while studying the cloudless sky.

"At least the pool should stay warm into the evening," Before fixing her eyes on me and adding, "You *are* staying for the show, aren't you, Alistair – and coming into the city after?"

I had planned nothing of the sort but nodded a clear acceptance.

We stopped before a large window beside the main entrance to the tea house, able to see within brightly coloured paper lanterns swinging from the ceiling above girls in just as brightly coloured and multi-layered dresses gliding gracefully over a matted floor, while maintaining expressionless faces under white powder, red lipstick, and jet-black hair in buns. These girls who must be the geishas were carrying trays of small tea pots and cups between low tables where principally male customers waited eagerly with bills in hand. A geisha noticed Annette and then gave a tilt of her head to the left.

"She wants us to go 'round the back, Alistair – You will try the sencha tea, won't you?"

I again nodded without any real choice before we proceeded to an area also screened off by bamboo at the rear of the tearoom. The only entrance to the hut was a screen door which emitted the occasional cloud of steam vapour. Annette waited by the door and then asked me straight.

"Are you sweet on Hortense?"

I was more than flabbergasted by the question and rendered temporarily mute.

*Was I?*

"No..." I tried to answer firmly hoping to leave no doubt in the questioner's mind, although there was still plenty left in mine, "We're good friends – she's more like a sister to me."

Annette nodded her head, "A boy could do worse."

Obviously not convinced by my response. The screen door then flew swiftly open and the geisha who had nodded to us poked her head outside, a needle in her hair grating the side of the screen.

"Hi Annie! Who yuh got 'ere?" Said the lady in a strong local drawl that belied her Asian appearance.

"This is Alistair, and he's from Mentone and I'm the lucky girl who gets to give him a tour."

"Well, bully for you, Annie." The geisha said as if perhaps kidding and then turned to me and bowed low. "Call me Lee, Alistair." Without prompting I played along, copying her bow, and replying as politely as I knew how, "Pleased to meet you, Lee."

"I bet you'd both like some tea. Give me two shakes an' I'll be back," With that the geisha disappeared back inside, Annette then asked.

"Where do you think Lee's from?"

"Japan, I suppose." Shrugging my shoulders.

"Lee's from Bendigo, and she's Chinese, but none of the customers would ever guess that. Who can speak Japanese around here anyway, or tell the difference in looks?"

With little knowledge of such things, I nodded my head in agreement.

"It's like a lot of things in the entertainment game – and life," Annette added, "They're just an illusion."

Lee returned and offered us two cups of tea, which we took from a tray and thanked her by giving a small bow as she went back inside. With caution I tasted the tea and found it passable, although I wouldn't be asking for a top up.

"How do you keep up with your studies?" I asked without thinking through my question, "You've got a lot on your plate 'round here." Annette appeared annoyed at my prying and then threw the dregs of her tea behind the hut and took my cup.

"There are no classes for what I do, Alistair," Annette said plainly then looked away and took moments to control a sadness that had swept over her face.

"I know I'll have to leave the girls." Annette paused after letting slip the French accent of her childhood, "...and this country." It was obvious that this was something weighing heavily on her mind, so I didn't intrude further.

"This show is a rage now," Annette said as her mood lightened, "but we'll see how it goes when the cold weather comes in. The public won't come out in the rain and watch someone swimming – It'll make 'em feel like peeing." Annette then gave me a broad grin.

"Let's go find the Cooblanna girls" She grabbed my arm and led me away.

*This is the most amazing day of my life!*

◄•►

# CHAPTER TEN

# 'Shooting the Chute'

"I BELIEVE A KISS is a window to the heart," Annette said as we strolled, leaning in and holding my arm tighter. "It will give you the answer."

I could feel a confidence growing within me by just having her near.

We passed a large wooden representation of a dragon and then skirted the sparkling man-made lake at the centre of the park. Annette and I then stopped and watched as an oarless boat flew down the giant water chute, patrons inside sent screaming as the vessel plunged deep into the lake's rippling surface, a spray of white water covering all on board.

*Did Annette know about my kiss with Horty – or Dorothy?*

In a way, it no longer mattered. I was enjoying my time with Annette for as long as it would last. She was showing me that the closeness of someone's company could be the most enjoyable thing in the world.

"Now, Alistair, seeing you are staying on for my show," I

nodded my head again, hoping her sister Mips had indeed told my folks that I might be late. "Then stand near the pontoon landing. It will give you the best viewing spot for my new act."

Annette then pointed and headed in the direction of a building with the words Café Chantant emblazoned across its façade; sets of small tables and chairs within brimming with customers. Beyond the café stood an open stage, where the attention of a large crowd was being captivated by the strange sight of a troupe of clowns dressed in loose white clothing with scattered black pom-poms attached, throwing themselves across the boards to the sound of a thumping piano.

I searched the crowd for Horty, or Abbie, or even Lucy Green, hoping they were among a throng of young people closer to the action.

"Hi Annette!" a piercing voice called out from behind, a second later a girl's hand forcibly gripped the arm opposite to the one entwined with mine. Immediately looking behind Annette, I could see it was no other than the girl who had forced me to kiss her last Saturday night: Dorothy.

Annette's body stiffened at this intrusion on her privacy, nodding with one sharp movement and then mouthing that she was about to let go of my arm. Dorothy pulled Annette slightly away from me and spoke to her alone.

"Despite the humid weather, the public have turned out to see you – haven't they? It must be wonderful to perform in front of an adoring crowd." Annette maintained her composure and replied without a hint of annoyance in her voice.

"I feel you will become accustomed to that quite soon." Annette replied. Dorothy beamed back a childish smile and then squeezed Annette's arm even tighter.

"Now Dorothy, shortly I will need you and some of the other girls to help me get into my costume and my new undergarment, brought to me kindly and in good time by Alistair here." Dorothy looked at me blankly and then her eyes shifted back to the side of Annette's face.

"Lucy and Abbie are down front – They won't be long; the Pierrots are on their final set."

*Don't worry where Horty is – You've just got the run of her house!*

While Dorothy hogged Annette's attention, I became intrigued by the frenetic jumping, rolling, and hip-hopping of the spotted seaside clowns. After the entire company had left to the rear of the stage, two returned to a rousing applause, one with a pile of white cone hats in hand, which he placed in a line in front of him, the other Pierrot came to a halt behind.

In unison and without words, they both did a hip-hop before the Pierrot in front turned a hat over using his foot and then flipped it onto his head, he then turned around and flipped it forward onto the head of his partner. In quick succession he flipped all hats from his head to the other, a hip-hop taking place between each turn.

The two Pierrots then faced each other and commenced to throw the hats onto the head of the opposite, increasing their speed until it became a blur, and finishing when each clown attained an equal number of hats. Not stopping to receive generous applause, they hopped into the next routine.

The Pierrots once again stood one behind the other. After a quick hip-hop the seaside clown in front placed a hat onto his head, did a full somersault, which released the hat at the top of his rotation, ending up landing squarely onto the head of his partner. With dash this partner then ran around to hand the hat back and made it back in time to trap the next twirling hat.

After they had completed the final somersault, the rest of the troupe joined the two performers, all then lined up arm in arm and sung a ditty not familiar to my ears.

*Some say we're dukes and marquises, perhaps we are, perhaps we're not.*

*But as I heard a lady say … Oh, that is just Pier – rot!*

To a monstrous round of applause, they exited the stage with each player performing a unique roll, hop, jump, or flip, to an extra cheer from the crowd. Out of the corner of my eye, I noticed the wave of a golden ribbon upon a straw hat, the girl wearing it, her face hidden by the brim, was being jostled along by the animated crowd. I waved hoping this girl would turn around so I could be certain who it was, but she was lost from my sight as the crowd surged towards the Café Charmant exit.

⤙•⤚

Down, down, down, the enormous water chute Annette slid, her silvery mermaid tail flapping high and shining bright in the late afternoon sun to feed the excitement of the crowd below. With her torso rolling like a wave, she slipped ever faster towards the spectators crammed six deep around the shimmering lake at the centre of Princes Court.

A din soon became a roar as clapping built to a crescendo in anticipation of Annette's entry into the clear water. Finally, she shot from the gigantic ramp and dove deep under the lake's surface leaving behind a stream of bubbles, resurfacing she skimmed in and out of the wake like a playful dolphin.

On the far side of the lake, Annette began to glide on her back, propelling herself along using the rhythmic wave of her tail to the cheers of the enthusiastic spectators who thrust their hands down trying to touch her shining body. The excited ruckus became louder as Annette approached the pontoon landing where I had secured a good vantage point, even though crammed in on all sides by onlookers.

Before the pontoon, Annette using sheer strength made her mermaid body rise out of the water. At the highest point two sailor-suited attendants placed oars under her arms and lifted her onto the landing where she splashed about before the spectators like a rampant harbour seal.

Two girls beside me squealed with fright and tried to move away from Annette, who no longer appeared of this world but more like a creature from the darkest depths of the ocean; long strands of material fell like seaweed from her body which now glowed like a ghostly apparition in the low sun.

Suddenly I felt skin rest against mine and gently I moved my arm away not wanting to become too familiar with strangers. However, as I turned my head, I saw a golden ribbon and knew it was Horty. She looked up at me with her cheeks full of excitement and gave me the warmest of smiles.

"Hi Loon," Horty whispered, "How wonderful is Annette – the Pierrots – everything?"

I returned her smile as the sailor assistants helped Annette onto her tail where she commenced to balance on her own before the crowd, at times threatening to launch herself forward which again sent a shriek of fear around the recoiling throng. Annette then raised her arms and shouted in a deep gurgling voice.

"Who will help me fly?"

Complete silence came over the stunned crowd, prompting Annette to shuffle even closer to the frightened audience.

Annette's voice then took on a witch's shrill, again calling the crowd into action.

"*Who* among you will help me fly?" Annette cajoling individuals with an outstretched arm.

"I will!" I shouted while raising an arm, Annette immediately acknowledged my interjection with a sharp nod. Soon after more joined in and cried 'I will!' 'I will!'.

"Then help me fly!" Annette shouted as her assistants shuffled her backwards to the edge of the pontoon. Spectators then broke into cries of 'Fly! – Fly! – Fly!' that built to a crescendo with the rise and fall of the pontoon, until finally Annette flung herself outwards from the landing, arching her back in mid-air like a crescent moon before entering the lake without a ripple, her body disappearing into a ring of silvery water.

The crowd waited in anticipation for Annette to resurface, until finally she appeared smoothly out of the water and waved her appreciation to the clapping audience. Once again, she skimmed the lake performing full twists and forward rolls to the delight of the cheering spectators, eventually being helped from the water by boat captains at the bottom of the water chute, who then spirited her away.

⟡

Horty grabbed my wrist, insistently dragging me in the direction of Annette's change-room. "C'mon Loon, we gotta get goin'!" Soon after we dodged either side of a young couple and came back together holding hands, "I said I'd help the girls get Annette outta her costume – I don't wanna miss out."

I went along with Horty's excitement, unable to believe two kids from a small village like Mentone knew the person who was the star of an incredible show. With Horty holding the straw hat firmly onto her head, and its golden ribbon bobbing in mid-air we ducked and weaved through the exhilarated crowd who had returned to wandering to all corners of the park.

"I wish I could've got Sniffle in as well!" Horty exclaimed through a cheeky grin, "He would've loved the show!"

*He would have – and thanks for thinking of us Horty Brown!*

Forgetting her surroundings, Horty continued to face me while heading straight for a lamppost that stood beside the lake. Instinctively, I used my spare hand to grab behind her elbow and pull her to a stop only a foot short of the post, her face inches from mine. I wanted to lean forward and kiss her right there and then. I wanted to desperately, but I wanted Horty to be the one to kiss me, so I knew for certain that I wasn't being a fool and that she did like me. After waiting too long for Horty to make the first move, I leant forward. She pulled her head back.

"Don't be silly Loon! – Can't be muckin' 'round now.

Quicker we get Annette changed the quicker we get to Collins Street."

Able to see Annette's change-room at the extremity of the park, we raced under the shadow of the water chute, Horty firmly holding my hand.

*Horty does like me!*

⁍•⁌

A group of patrons had already gathered around the door of Annette's change-room, where Alfred with arms stretched wide was struggling to hold them back. Horty politely pushed through the crowd until she reached the minder, who had to be reminded that they had made their acquaintance three or four times this week. After a brief deliberation, Alfred let us go through to the door where Horty gave three sharp wraps and said hastily to me.

"Wait here Loon. Prob'ly nearly done anyway."

Seconds later the door opened only inches wide, and Dorothy's face peered out and instantly gave me the coldest look before she opened the door only a foot wider to let Horty squeeze in. As I turned around, I felt the heavy gaze of the crowd upon me, perhaps wondering why a young man was standing outside Annette's change-room door looking nervously out of place. To ease my discomfort, I gradually shuffled along the change-room wall until it met the public lavatories and then slipped into the gap between.

231

The aqua-blue door of Annette's change-room suddenly opened, and a gasp went up from her patiently waiting fans. To their disappointment and to an extent mine, Dorothy appeared out of the room, not with something to say to the patrons but solely to look around until she saw me standing between buildings. She strode towards me in a direct line, the look on her face no better than when she first opened the door. Stopping before me she blurted out.

"Horty tells me you're coming with the *girls* to Collins Street – Is that true?"

Taking my time, I replied with the manners she was failing to show me.

"Hello Dorothy. Annette asked me to come along, and Horty's happy I go, but if you don't want me to go. I won't."

"Listen Alistair..." Dorothy stopped herself and glared harder, seething with an anger I failed to understand.

"We are not just going to Collins Street. Annette is shouting the Follity girls – *Follity girls!* – to the Paris Café to thank them for getting her changed before and after each show. You do one thing and expect to come along."

"I do not *expect* anything Dorothy. I said I wouldn't go if you didn't want me to." My anger beginning to match hers.

Dorothy turned back to look at the change-room door and then returned to me.

"Alistair, Horty will never say anything to hurt you – but

I will – for your own good – and hers. If you come with us to the Paris Café, it will ruin everything. The girls won't be able to talk freely, and we *will* be talking about boys. And now that I mention it, a boy named Callum from McCristal's school likes her and her face lights up every time we mention his name."

Dorothy then pointed with aggression at my face and said just holding down her voice.

"I'm telling you right now, Alistair, you are both too young to settle – My parents met at your age and now they're miserable – Do the right thing and leave her be!"

Dorothy had stunned me into silence with those words and I said nothing when she touched the side of my cheek gently, turned on the spot and then returned to the change-room door that had just opened.

*She knows nothing! – I can't leave Horty be – She's my best friend!*

—•◦—

Appearing in the frame of the door with one arm stretched high, her body elongated to show off a shimmering sea-green dress, Annette then waved as she stepped confidently towards the crowd, both her hands soon touching and holding those of her admirers. After giving sufficient time to each devotee, Annette raised her hands high and took a step back.

"I am so happy you enjoyed the show. I tried something different this evening and I hope it was a success."

A warm round of applause went up and a man shouted 'sure was' from the back of the crowd. Horty by then was by my side and I greeted her with a cheerful smile, even though I had to force myself not to repeat what Dorothy had said.

"Ready Loon?" Horty said, as she wrapped fingers around my arm, "Annette's so nice, she's takin' us to the Paris Café in the city – So generous!"

Horty moved off, but I held my ground. Horty pulled up as our arms stretched out.

"Comin'?" she asked, a query on her face about my reluctance. I delayed replying for as long as I could, no longer clear about anything after what Dorothy had said. She was right about the Follity girls not wanting me hanging around on their special evening – but what I really needed now was time to think everything through.

Without giving away my dilemma, I had to think up something in seconds flat that would get me away from here – from Horty – from Dorothy – from everybody – as soon as I could.

"Hort, I'm gonna let you and the girls go on yuh own." I said barely able to get the words out because of the embarrassment I was feeling.

"I'm gettin' on well with Dad at the moment an' he's startin' tuh show me how tuh work the farm," The lie surely apparent on my face, "He wants me tuh get up early t'morra an' help him."

"You girls deserve a treat for what you've done. Tell me what went on when yuh get back home."

Horty eyes never left mine and I could feel her fingers tightening around my arm.

"Did Dorothy say something?" Horty asked quietly but insisting on the truth, "I saw her touch your face."

*Bloody hell!*

I had to continue with the lies, there was no other way out of this. "She was just bein' silly. We were talkin' about the creepy material on Annette's costume."

Horty gently took her hand away from my arm, still studying my eyes.

"She better not have said anything about us – bloody floozy!"

I had to stop this conversation and leave before things went any further. I didn't want an ugly fight to start between Horty and Dorothy. It would make life too diffi-cult for all concerned.

"Nothing was said Hort, honest. Enjoy the café – and can yuh please say thanks to Annette for me?"

Horty nodded her head, and although there was still uncertainty in her eyes she swung around on the balls of her feet to notice that Annette and her entourage were now well on their way to the St Kilda Road exit. As she strode away, Horty turned back, a smile belatedly returning to her face.

"Better catch 'em up Loon. See yuh when I get home."

After collecting my thoughts, I found myself alone with Alfred, who took great pleasure in giving me the stare and pointing a stubby finger in the direction of the nearest exit.

—•—

# CHAPTER ELEVEN

# Leaving Her Be

## MID-APRIL 1905

"YOU ARE BEING SO rude, Loon – I can hardly believe it!"

With that I crouched even lower behind the gnarly and twisted tea-tree lying close to the ground at the bottom of our lower paddock, not a great distance from Beach Road.

"I saw you head off down here when you noticed Horty on the porch."

Millie placed clenched fists on her hips, allowing her apron to swing either side of her body in the freshening onshore breeze. She kept trying to pick me out against the thick outcrop of tea-tree, melaleuca, and she-oak, where I had headed in panic on seeing someone who I desperately wanted to talk to, but couldn't, because of the words Dorothy had shouted at me at Princes Court, words which had dominated my every thought since then, until finally convincing me that they may be right.

*But I don't know what right or wrong is anymore*

"Why are you doing this? Horty was looking forward to telling you all about her time at Cooblanna. You have no consideration for anyone lately – but lucky I do. I told her you weren't back home from school yet ... and Mum and Dad are just as fed up as me."

Millie made one more sweep of the scrub before giving up and storming off towards home, reminding me as she went, "You're gonna get a bloody earful from all of us when you come in for tea."

I made sure Millie had gone before I sat myself down dejected on the trunk of the tea-tree. I put both hands over my face wanting to cry but couldn't.

*I don't want to hurt anybody!*

My need to get away from everyone recently had become overwhelming. I didn't want to talk to anyone at school, where I couldn't concentrate anyway, and Sniffle chided me for not turning up to walk with him to school and then avoided me all day. I didn't even want to do my bakery round tomorrow, even if it was Mr Hall's last Saturday.

The only one who didn't care if I spoke to him or not was Perce, who said I'd 'start talkin'' after I'd seen Manning's new gelding tomorrow afternoon and then gone for a ride in the motor car that had been advertised to be at McCristal's Mentone College garden fete, where the whole town and a 'great number' of visitors were expected to turn out to get a closer look at the latest wonder of science.

Going to see the new gelding might be fine, but I didn't

think I could be around the masses of people expected at McCristals.

I would apologize to Mum, Dad, and Millie as soon as I got back inside, but I wouldn't be able to tell them when I would be my old self again, because I didn't know. I wished in a way that I had never gone to Princes Court, then I wouldn't have had to hear the words 'do the right thing and leave her be', because right now, I wanted to let everybody be.

The only thing I wanted to do was sleep, and in the vivid dreams that followed the faces of girls I knew appeared; Felicity, Abbie Taylor, and Lucy Green among others, and although I disliked Dorothy, it was her I kissed in every slumber – not Horty. I would never be able to talk to anyone about these things, certainly not Horty, nor my closest friends, and not even Mum and Dad, or Millie. I had to work this out on my own.

◆•◆

I apologized to Mum, Dad, and Millie when I went back inside for tea, which they accepted more graciously than I expected and after picking at my food around a quiet kitchen table asked if I could be excused to go to bed.

◆•◆

The next morning, I was shocked to see Dad's face above

and close to mine and feeling his strong hands shaking my shoulders; only a moment before I heard two words.

"Get! – Up!"

Even after splashing my face with icy water, I was still half asleep when Dad shoved an unsoaked bowl of porridge in front of me, Mum's honey the only saving grace. I was grateful for Dad waking me, and I told him so, as I was most likely to have slept well into the morning, then there would have been no end of trouble with Mr Hall and Mr Rennie, even if he did wake me in the middle of an enjoyable dream with three of my regular visitors.

—•—

Dad went even further out of his way to make sure I didn't run off and hide by dropping me off at the bakery lane in his buggy and then staying on to watch me walk in through the stable doors.

With trepidation as to how Mr Hall would be feeling about being pushed out of his lucrative Saturday round, I yelled out 'Mornin', but my fears were soon allayed when I heard Geoffrey on the other side of Clopper, whistling to himself as he fastened his reins and lines and was still humming as I walked gingerly up to him.

I was ready for disgruntled words, but Mr Hall said calmly that he had almost finished loading the back, and that he would cart the bulk of the deliveries today. In shock with this unexpected change in behaviour and still wary that it may not last the whole round, we headed out onto Florence Street with Geoffrey recommencing to whistle cheerfully, which was annoying in its own way.

At most drops Mr Hall had his notebook out and scribbled down whispered names, while at other drops he presented a card. To my mind, he was still in the same game but only changing location as I overheard the odd person say they would catch up with him at Dempsey's track or Mentone Racecourse. I figured this may have been something he had wanted to do for a long time and was quietly thankful for the final push. At the end of the round which had me frequently dozing off with little to do, Mr Geoffrey Hall said he hoped to see me at the track if I was still interested, and even though we continued to share the same stables, I was glad we had parted on reasonable terms.

⸭

When I arrived back home a little after midday, I went to see Dad in the lower paddock and thanked him again for helping me get to work in the morning. He said that after lunch the rest of the family would be getting ready for the fete and that if I felt up to it I could join them to pick up the Browns and Lucia at La Plage, and then walk to McCristals. I asked if he could give me a little time to think about it, so he nodded and left for the house.

As my thoughts were much clearer after the bakery round, and it was a beautiful autumn day, I figured that I might be able to join my friends at the fete, and that included seeing if I could talk to Horty somewhere, which would likely be at one of the stalls run by the Mentone Girls' School.

—•—

Even before Dad had made it back inside, I had already decided that it was time for me to end my selfish exile and join the family in what could be a fun day at McCristals. I was slowly walking up the slight rise back to my house when I heard Perce call loudly.

"You're in for it now Loon!"

I turned to face the sound and then felt air rush from my lungs as my chest gave way under the full force of Perce's low and bent shoulder. He had knocked me off my feet and was now grinding me into the loose damp soil of the lower paddock. Dizziness and confusion came over me as I quickly tried to figure out why this was happening. I then felt hands holding my shoulders down and looked up to see Perce's grimaced face above me.

"I told Manning's boys you're as good as gold – never late I told 'em – They held up the trial of their new gelding for ten minutes – ten bloody minutes! – for you! – but yuh didn't show!"

*Shit! – I went past Dempsey's twice – only three hours ago!*

Perce then released his right hand and slapped me across the top of my head.

"Perce, I'm sorry, I clean forgot."

"Shut up, Loon! I saw yuh wagon go past early." Was all I got back before he shouted.

"Yuh said last Sunday you'd come – yuh promised!"

"Perce – I ain't been right." To which he shook his head.

"Nuh! Yuh can't treat yuh mates like yuh been doin' – Yuh can't stiff yuh mates and get away with it. Sniff was waitin' tuh walk tuh school with yuh, t' show yuh the agates he won from a new kid – An' yuh prob'ly done somethin' wrong tuh Horty as well."

Perce released the pressure off my shoulders which allowed me to sit up and see Sniffle standing uneasily ten yards away.

"I ought a' clobber yuh with a couple of gooduns for what yuh done – but it wouldn't do any good because yuh don't care about anyone but yaself."

Perce stood and then started to walk back to Sniffle who had turned his face away, unable to look me in the eye.

"You're the one who's got it wrong Perce," I shouted loud enough so he knew I was serious, "Good friends don't give up on their mates – they give 'em time tuh sort 'emselves out! So, you're the one who's not a good mate!" Perce and Sniffle ignored me and kept walking away.

"Come here Perce and I'll knock yuh bloody head off!"

Perce stopped and slowly turned around before striding

steadily towards me. He had already produced a tight fist by the time he reached me and threw it at my head with force. But if I had learnt one thing from the fight with Loz it was that you had to anticipate what was coming next. I dodged low to my right and landed a decent left fist into Perce's stomach which winded him enough to make him drop to his knees.

I thought that may be enough to make him think twice about continuing his carry on, but Perce was not ready to call it quits. With his long reach he swung his left arm back and around my lowered neck, managing to take me in a headlock and pull me down on my knees. In the distance I could see Sniffle knocking on the door of our back porch, shortly before Perce gave me a sharp punch into the ribs with his loose right hand. This fight was to have no winner so I tried to stand and call a truce, but Perce would not let go of my neck or stop punching my side.

With one final effort, I thrust Perce backwards severely bending his knees and making him cry out for me to stop. Suddenly, I was lifted straight up in the air by an unseen force at the same time as I could see the raised veins of a muscular arm grab Perce by the front of his shirt. Within seconds Perce and I were facing each other with Dad holding firmly onto both of us.

"Now, don't any one of you dare say the other started this – I won't have it!" Dad shook us to make sure we understood. I managed to glance behind Dad to see Millie holding Mum's arm with Sniffle standing alongside, all with shocked looks on their faces.

"First thing you two are going to do is shake each other's hands and say sorry to your mate."

Perce stubbornly shook his head and then looked away. I pursed my lips not wanting to do it.

"Do it!" Dad said firmly to me through gritted teeth and then glared at Perce. I moved my hand out and positioned it ready for Perce, who slowly stretched out his arm until our hands met and we had a quick shake, saying 'sorry' at the same time.

"That's better – Now Alistair you are going to apologize to anyone you've wronged lately, and that includes the person you were rude to yesterday."

Dad released his grip on both our shirts and relaxed his stance.

"Now you three boys are going to get ready for this afternoon's fete and meet each other outside McCristals and walk in together as mates – or Perce and Neville, don't bother showing your faces around this part of the world again."

Dad looked around to see Sniffle already nodding his head and then back to Perce who gave one quick nod of his.

"Now get outta my sight, both of you!" Dad pushed Perce and I away from each other and walked back to join Mum and Millie who had already started walking back towards the house.

◆•◆

# CHAPTER TWELVE

# McCristal's Garden Party and Children's Fete

## MID-APRIL 1905

**SNIFFLE WAS THE FIRST** to join me near the ticket box at the bottom of the tree-lined drive at the Beach Road entrance to McCristal's Mentone College. Before he had a chance to say anything I apologized for not turning up to walk to school with him last week, which he accepted with a simple nod of his head, and then we shook hands. Dad who was standing alone in the shadows beside the entrance to the Mentone Hotel, watched our every movement with interest, making sure we fulfilled our promise. I had little doubt that Sniffle would show up, Perce was more likely not to.

I wasn't a fool; I knew by my recent behaviour that two of my best mates had lost a large degree of faith in me; I couldn't bear to lose the trust of the other.

Predictions were right as a stream of locals and a good number of visitors were now pouring through the open gates, making Sniffle and I become a little concerned at Perce's lateness. We could see lines already forming in front of brightly decorated stalls and an especially long one waiting to take a ride in the motor car, currently performing a smoky circuit of the sports field.

Fortunately, Perce showed up only seconds before Sniffle and I finished counting down a final minute. He put on a cheery front and then shook Sniffle and my hands, turning at such an angle to make sure Dad saw the event before urging us to go in together. No sooner had we paid our sixpence and were walking down the drive than Perce pointed to an animated group of people forming a circle on the far side of Salisbury Street, close to the alley that housed the bulk of the produce stalls and sideshows.

"Ave a look at that!" Perce gasped as he turned to make sure Sniffle and I were aware,

"There's a bloke over there walkin' around with no clothes on – in a barrel!"

Perce took a couple more strides then turned and waved to Sniffle.

"Comin' Sniff?"

My heart sank on realizing the damage I had done in the previous week. I fully expected Sniffle to walk away, but to my surprise and great relief he held his ground and while maintaining an expressionless face said calmly to Perce.

"Nuh, me and Loon are gonna try and find Horty first – See yuh later on."

Perce, after glaring at Sniffle for an extended amount of time, turned his back on us and walked steadily towards the sideshow commotion. I could do no more than place a hand on Sniffle's shoulder – more grateful for those words than any others in my life.

—•—

Near the end of the drive, Sniffle tapped me on the shoulder and pointed towards a marquee to the right of the former Davies' family mansion, currently being used for school administration and student lodgings. Spread across the vast lawn in front of the elegant building were fashionable ladies and gentlemen seated around small tables while being served afternoon tea by young ladies with white pinafores over their dark blue waitress dresses.

"There's the Cooblanna girls!" he exclaimed, "They must be doin' high tea!"

Even at a distance, I could see Principal Sampson standing in full sunlight outside a marquee brightly decorated in eucalypt and banksia blooms, directing three of her young charges where to take trays of terraced sandwiches and cakes to the correct patrons. One of the waitresses was Dorothy, who went directly to fuss about at a table where two young men were seated.

I searched within the vicinity until I found Horty standing on her own inside a stall closer to the main hubbub of the fete selling cupcakes topped with glacé cherries to predominantly young eager children.

"I'm gonna see how my dad's goin' in the Aunt Sally," Sniffle said with expected pride, "Yuh know how much he loves it. This year he even put a dolly up in the backyard."

I was listening to Sniffle but only taking in half of what he was saying as my attention had been drawn to a person striding across the lawn and through the turned heads of the seated patrons. I strained my eyes to make sure it was the same person who I thought it was, a person who I would have sworn wouldn't feel comfortable either attending a garden party or taking part in the light-hearted entertainment on offer at a children's fete.

*Perhaps Loz wants a ride in the motor car.*

"Whadayuh reckon he's up to Loon?" Sniffle asked on realizing Loz was heading directly towards Horty's stall, "I'm gonna wait until he clears off."

"Dunno what he's doin' here Sniff, but he won't try anythin' with Constable Canty around,"

*And why isn't Roscoe with him!*

"I'll go and find out what he's up to, Sniff," I said to reassure him, "D'yuh want me tuh grab yuh a cupcake while I'm there?"

Sniffle nodded his head and then let me know some of his thoughts on Loz.

"Just watch that bugger. He let us off the hook during the fishin' trip, but he's never done anyone a favour before that."

Sniffle had another look over to where the Aunt Sally was being held, "...and don't jabber on too long with Horty, the motor car line's gettin' long ... I'll keep a spot for yuh."

"Thanks Sniff, won't be long." I guaranteed and then added as I took off in my own direct line towards Horty and her surprise visitor, "I'll say hello to Horty for yuh."

By the time I arrived at the cake stall, two girls were waiting patiently behind Loz, who in an exaggerated manner was throwing his arms about while curling his wrists displaying to Horty how to do something, who in turn seemed engrossed in every motion and every word he said. She then sensed that the girls in front of me may be getting neglected and told them she would get to them soon. Before she returned to Loz, Horty gave me a lukewarm smile.

Once Loz had finished his display, Horty placed a hand on top of his and whispered words that I failed to pick up. Loz squeezed her hand and then spoke briefly before he strode off towards Salisbury Street at the same pace as he had arrived, leaving the college grounds without so much as a curious look at any attraction. I was intrigued as to what he could have been speaking to Horty about – but at the same time – glad that he had gone.

"Hi Hort – Wha'd Loz want?"

Horty folded her arms and glared disappointedly at me. I didn't think I had said anything wrong but then had to remind myself that I had been acting in a strange and selfish manner lately, and that perhaps I should stop and think about what I was about to say, before shooting my mouth off.

"Sorry Hort – Did yuh have a good time at Cooblanna?" I asked, scrambling to recover from a bad start, "...the Paris Café must a' been great?"

"By the way, Sniffle says hello."

Horty relaxed her arms and gave me a warmer smile, she then looked behind me to make sure no-one was waiting.

"The Paris Café was so much fun. The food and service was incredible. We laughed our heads off all evening – until we got the bill – which was outrageous! All the girls had to empty out their purses to help Annette pay for it – Still, it was the best night ever."

Horty then looked strangely at me, in the same way as she had at the red desert, which seemed so long ago now.

"I missed you yesterday," Horty said losing her smile, "but I knew you were there."

*We know each other too well – That's the problem*

"Loz came to say goodbye and apologize again for the fight. He's headin' up north to find work. He says it doesn't feel like home to him around here anymore."

"That's silly..."

"No, it's not Loon!" Horty emphasised with a shake of

her head, "Did yuh see the way people looked at him? – He gets that every day!"

*Horty was right – It didn't matter what Loz did – he would never get a fair go here*

I nodded my head and then asked just on the off chance.

"Do yuh wanna go fishin' now yuh back – There's plenty around."

"I'd like to, Loon, but the Follity Club's gotta partner with the McCristal boys to put on a show to raise money for the Convalescent Home for Men in Cheltenham – Miss Ellie wasn't happy with our last performance – I thought it was good."

*I'm sure Horty's eyes will light up if Master Callum is made her partner*

I was tempted to ask Horty about her favourite student at McCristals, not having heard of a Callum at the school, or any other school in the area for that matter. But, unless I wanted Horty to think I was jealous of him, it was best to say nothing.

"I'd better go, Hort. Sniffle's keepin' a spot for me in the motor car line." I said, happy to leave with our friendship intact. I moved to step away, but stopped as I could hear a lad behind me say something about the girl 'takin' forever'. I ignored this comment as a sharp pain in my ribs reminded me of my recent fight with Perce.

While I was distracted Horty had returned to filling plates with glacé cherry cupcakes perhaps glad I was soon to move on. Again, I heard the same lad say, "She's so slow!". Within a split second I had swung around and shouted.

"Why don't you shut your smart mouth!"

My outburst shocked me as there were two boys facing me; one around ten years of age, who went silent and froze on the spot and another of perhaps five years of age who was already crying as he took a frightened step away from me. I turned back to Horty who also had a shocked look on her face.

*What the hell is wrong with me?*

"Sorry," I said immediately to Horty and then returned to the two boys to apologize,

"Sorry lads, I shouldn't a' yelled," Then tried to think of some way to make up for my bad behaviour. "What if I buy yuh a cupcake each?"

The older boy however would have nothing to do with my offer and grabbed his shaking brother by the arm and led him away in the direction of the sideshow alley.

"Me brother just wanted a cupcake, that's all." He added to make me feel worse than I already did. I lowered my head not wanting to turn back and face Horty.

"They weren't sayin' anything that bad, Loon." Horty said, staring at me curiously as if I was someone she had never seen before.

I felt so embarrassed that Horty had to witness me act so aggressively. I thought I was over my selfish antics. All I could do was somehow try to explain and then do as Dorothy had told me and leave her be.

"I dunno what's got into me lately Hort. I really don't. I get either angry or sleepy at the drop of a hat – and act stupid pretty-well all the time – Might be better if I headed up north with Loz."

To my surprise Horty shook her head and a smirk formed, apparently finding my latest comment amusing.

"Yuh'd kill each other within a week, Loon ... be fun to watch, though!"

Horty's response partially shook me out of the doldrums.

"Don't worry, everyone's actin' a bit strange lately ... me too, I'm told."

Horty handed me two cupcakes while I returned a thankful smile for her understanding.

"Sniffle will like the cupcakes, they're nice and sweet – Go on, get goin' and enjoy the ride – I went earlier – it was amazin'!"

Horty then waved me away with both hands.

"See yuh down the sideshow alley if I ever get finished here."

—•—

"C'mon kids, don't push in. I know who's next in line." Shouted Mr Ruby, the college's caretaker and the man in charge of the order in which patrons were allowed on board the modern wonder that was the motor car.

The two wide line of predominantly children waiting for

a ride stretched from over Salisbury Street to the loading point halfway to Beach Road. With the start of the ride only yards from the main drive, the adults strolling past could be seen looking down their noses at the smoky vehicle with handkerchiefs over their mouths, pretending not to be interested in this incredible invention that was likely to change their lives in unimaginable ways.

I pushed Sniffle forward to make him push the two boys in front of him closer to the idling motor vehicle, which was shuddering and rocking from side to side while belching fumes from a rear pipe and under the engine cover. What encouraged me to move Sniffle and myself forward and to not turn around either, was that the girl behind me I knew to be the bane of our class at Cheltenham State School: Rene Marshall.

Rene had earned that title because of her tendency to cry and throw herself to the floor at the slightest hint of criticism or scream and dob a schoolmate into the teacher if they so much as said boo to her, and although she had been away for three weeks visiting relatives, I still didn't want to acknowledge she was there.

Mr Ruby, who was also McCristal's sports master, stretched out an arm after letting five children pass through and stopped the two boys in front of Sniffle and me at a makeshift gate only yards away from the motor vehicle that now appeared more like a loud and reeky beast in comparison to a fine horse-drawn carriage, and had a few people questioning whether this latest invention would be the ruin of mankind or a godsend to put an end to the tediousness of travel beyond the train line.

The motor car once loaded with its five passengers, then shuddered away over sunken timber and split logs laid down to protect the soft sports field surface for its promised run from 'one end of town to the other'. After rumbling over corrugated ruts in Salisbury Street, the car turned a sharp right into Palermo Street and was lost in a cloud of smoke.

—•—

"What sort of motor car is it Mr Ruby?" Sniffle asked as soon as he had settled in front of the caretaker's ample paunch.

"First time I've been asked *that* today, Neville," Mr Ruby grinned sarcastically.

"It's an Argyll. Made in Scotland. It has four cylinders with a T gate, speed change levers, and a separate reversing box ... It's a marvellous automobile."

*What was that...?*

—•—

Excitement grew among the soon to be boarding as we saw the motor vehicle turning from Mentone Parade into Palermo Street and then make a right into Salisbury Street where it again shuddered over ruts and rumbled over submerged logs, coming to a halt before us. As the excited passengers pushed past us, they could be heard breathlessly saying.

"That was so great!" "Thought I'd be scared..." "Should go again!"

Once Mr Ruby had opened the makeshift gate, we raced over to the shaking rear compartment of the open to the air horseless carriage, where I settled snuggly in beside Sniffle, who had shoved the other two boys across the seat, one who may have wet his pants. I waited and hoped that it hadn't been Rene who was squeezing in beside me, but I knew by glancing at a faded navy-blue dress and yellowing white frilly hat, that it couldn't be anyone else.

"Hi Loon! – Isn't this exciting?" Rene said in her deceptively quiet as a mouse voice while perched at an awkward angle halfway up the seat's leather stitching, allowing just enough room for Mr Ruby to press the door closed; her bare lower leg then resting against mine.

*I bet she's gonna scream or blubber for the whole trip!*

"Hi Rene," I eventually got back, "Haven't seen yuh 'round lately,"

"Been visitin' cousins..." Rene replied quickly, without feeling the need to say where.

The driver gave a couple of quick revs of the engine, leant an arm over the driver's seat and then spoke through a fixed smile and with a cultured British accent to his five passengers.

"Hello kids, I'm Mr Ross from Tarrant Motors and I hope you are going to enjoy your little jaunt today in my favourite automobile: Betsy." The driver then pulled goggles down from the top of his leather cap and secured them over his eyes.

"Now, can I ask you to give Betsy a little help to get going – Are you ready!"

Having heard this cheer repeated a dozen times as we crept closer to Mr Ruby, we knew exactly what to yell. As the motor car rolled off, we screamed together. "Go Betsy!"

Shuddering over Salisbury Street, the engine revved high, and vibrations were sent through the vehicle to our already shaking bodies.

Before anyone in the rear was ready, the motor vehicle braked and turned a sharp right into Palermo Street. I was forced sideways, my face pressing into Sniffle's sleeve, seconds later I was thrown in the opposite direction as we turned left into Naples Road, my shoulder pressing up against Rene's; the rag curls of her ponytail tickling my neck as we turned another right into Lucerne Street.

*I think I'm gonna be sick*

Thankfully, the vehicle then straightened to run parallel to the railway line along Como Parade and I had to suffer Rene telling me about how her brother Luke, and Bert and Cec Young, would be chaperoning her and her only friend, Rita Coule, to the Coles Book Arcade in the city, next Saturday.

It was always a matter of curiosity to see Rene and Big Luke standing beside each other at school while also knowing that they were siblings, where the huge amount of contrasts in their appearance and attitude had many wondering about their parentage; Rene was nervous and petite with strawberry-blonde straight hair, with a tendency to break down in tears at any second, whereas a year older Luke had a resolute manner backed with a solid build, a mop of dark curly hair, thick black eyebrows, and the makings of an early beard.

Along Como Parade, Mr Ross turned his head slightly and then shouted.

"What's that building on the left kids?"

In unison we shouted, "The R. C. Church, Mr Ross." While all this was going on, I couldn't help but notice that Rene had changed – for the better – her face could now be called pretty, her figure quite shapely.

Sniffle then leant over, poked me in the side and whispered.

"Why yuh talkin' to Rene for, Loon? – You'll end up gettin' in trouble for somethin'."

*In trouble for what Sniff?*

Mr Ross then slowed, and I prepared myself for another left turn at Balcombe Road. Once again, I was forced close to Rene, close enough to smell her overly sweet perfume and to hear her whisper as her lips had ended up close to my ear.

"Loon, it's past our kissin' time."

*Kissin' time! – No, it ain't, Rene! ... Not on yuh Nelly!*

Along Balcombe Road, the motor vehicle overtook traps and buggies that swayed in jerky movements out of our way. We continued along Balcombe until the corner of Elizabeth Street, where I tried to count the number of turns we might have left before we made it back to McCristals, but lost count when we slipped into Valencia Street. At the bottom of that tight and muddy lane, we turned left into Brindisi Street and the three other boys shouted to Mr Ross, "There's the Gas Works, Mr Ross." In the meantime, Rene had stayed close to my ear while remaining safely hidden from Sniffle's view.

"Loon, I want you to be the first boy I kiss." She whispered, this time rubbing her bare lower leg against mine.

*What! Why me? Can't someone else do it – Anyone!*

Rene kept rubbing my leg and I could feel her warm breath against the side of my face as we went over a small bump entering Mentone Parade, and all I could hope for was a quick end to this trip.

*S'pose I could do it if she doesn't want another – and why not, I'm sure Horty will be kissin' Callum as soon as she can!*

"After school Monday, Rene," I whispered with my head turned slightly in her direction, "Meet me under the ghost tree next tuh the cemetery – On yuh own!"

"Don't worry, Loon. I know what to do, you'll see – I read about it in a book my cousins had." Rene then blew warm breath into my ear, and I suddenly felt an empty feeling in my stomach and tingling in my groin.

*God no! – It can't be happenin' here!*

Mr Ross then revved the engine and sped down Mentone Parade with all but me waving and shouting to a line of latecomers heading towards Mentone College. In pain I crossed my legs as we turned into Salisbury Street and rumbled over corrugated ruts, all the while trying to figure out how I was going to clear the hidden log obstacle at the end of the ride.

The one obstacle I wasn't expecting today.

—•••—

After the effects of the motor car ride had eased, I managed to beat Sniffle in most games in the sideshow alley off Salisbury Street, except the pyramid of cans where Sniffle had the handy knack of picking out the weighted can and knocking it down in his first throw. Sniffle was handed a sad looking rag doll for his trouble which he offloaded quick-smart to a young girl behind him in line. We were having so much fun together that I barely had time to think about Perce, or Horty.

Our next attempt at a dubious prize was at the apple bobbing tank, which Sniffle took to with unsurprising fervour, requiring the attendant to shuffle him along to the next attraction. We were running out of interesting games to try when we saw the red and white striped Punch and Judy booth and could hear a show in full swing on the vacant lawn before the classroom block.

We stood at the back of an engrossed crowd spread out on picnic rugs, laughing at every whack the Constable received from Mr Punch's slapstick and every grimace the Bottler made at the side of the booth. Sniffle then discreetly tugged at my sleeve and pointed to the far right of the gathering and a person who sat alone: Millie.

It was expected that after Millie entered the grounds with Mum and the Browns that she would be joined by the man who had accompanied her to dances and charity events in the last month. A man I had my doubts about in the beginning but could find no proof to base my dislike upon. The closer we got to Millie it was obvious she had been crying as her head was lowered, her eyes red, and she was holding a crumpled white handkerchief in one hand.

*What has that bastard done?*

Sniffle put a hand on my chest and told me not to budge from the back of the crowd. He could see my cheerful grin had change to clenched teeth within seconds, my hands starting to shake.

"Stay here, Loon!" Sniffle ordered and then walked around the crowd towards Millie often peeking back to make sure I was doing as I was told. When he reached Millie, he took a deep breath and then sat down beside her, not saying a word or turning his face from the show.

Millie looked at Sniffle, contemplating what his arrival was about and then thirty seconds later, leant her head against his shoulder. I had been underestimating Sniffle all my life, taking his hesitant gentle nature as a form of weakness, yet here he was, the right person Millie needed right now.

After only a minute Sniffle gave me a sign to come over and sit on the other side of Millie. I copied what Sniffle had done and soon after Millie held my arm and turned to me.

"He said I wasn't the right girl for him, Loon," Millie then took short sharp breaths, "...but I was."

I was angry, but also beginning to understand how fraught with danger growing up could be, and getting hurt from time to time was an unavoidable part of it. I wouldn't say anything foolish about finding this man and challenging him to a fight – one was enough for today – and besides, Millie deserved someone so much better than him.

As the sun dipped behind and made a silhouette of the Mentone Hotel, a cool breeze sprung up and followed the long shadows creeping across the Mentone College's playing field to the classroom block lawn and adjacent sideshow alley. At the end of the Punch and Judy show, the outrageous beatings and hilarious antics had managed to cheer Millie up a tad, and the makings of a smile was evident.

After a short walk through the game's alley, Millie said she wanted to go home, and as Mum, Dad, and the Browns had left earlier after Samuel had become overwhelmed by the occasion, Sniffle and I decided that we might as well leave as well so that Millie didn't have to walk home on her own.

◆•◆

What had been a trickle of people leaving the fete an hour earlier, had turned into a steady exodus of principally tired-eyed and grumpy children cajoled by their parents to stop dawdling and keep moving down the college drive towards the entrance at Beach Road, which was now its major exit.

Twenty yards from this exit, I could hear the strangely familiar sound of feet pounding on gravel coming from behind. I swung around just in time to see Horty throw her arms over Millie and Sniffle's shoulders and then add so that Sniffle and I were aware.

"Thanks for waitin' for me fellas!"

"Hi Horty," Millie and Sniffle replied with a noticeable lack of enthusiasm. Horty then looked quizzically over at me wondering what their down looks were about. I nodded my head in Millie's direction as we cleared the college gates, trying to think of a way to let Horty know that she had been jilted, but no expression existed that could go close to explaining that.

After Millie, Horty, and Sniffle had stepped out onto Beach Road, I stopped and looked back down the drive with a foolish hope that I would see Perce running franti-cally to catch up with us. I spent a full minute searching the grounds for a sign of him, then raced to catch up to my sister and our friends.

—•—

Millie's mood lifted even further as Horty told her the mildly amusing story about how Dorothy had been showing off at her birthday celebrations and managed to get toffee all through her hair, ending up with Principal Sampson standing over her cutting out tangled clumps while berating her with a large pair of tailor's scissors in hand.

Then in silence, we marched happily towards our homes enjoying the warm glow of the sun on our faces as it sat just above the curve of Beach Road; Horty's arms still over Millie and Sniffle's shoulders, which left me to walk behind, so grateful to have each of them in my life.

Then for no apparent reason, Horty pulled up sharply, took her arms off Millie and Sniffle's shoulders and put a finger up to her lips. Initially we were bemused by her sudden actions, until she used her pointer to draw our attention to a thicket of deep green melaleuca entangled with tea-tree and partially screened by the russet fronds of she-oak. Horty then ran fingers along her arm to indicate there was an animal within the undergrowth. We followed the direction of her arm and looked intently for any sign of movement.

Sniffle and Millie stepped stealthily forward over low bracken before shaking their heads to indicate they could see no animal. Horty and I were a half dozen steps behind when I noticed movement within the thicket and what I was certain was a set of spots above the branch of a tea-tree close to the sharp drop at the edge of the slopes. The animal as if aware that it was being watched disappeared into dark leafy shadows and was lost from my sight.

Sniffle and Millie were now wanting to give up, but I continued to point towards the patch of deep green only yards ahead of them. We waited in silence and without movement even as buggies and carriages carrying loud and lively passengers slipped by on Beach Road.

Less than a minute later and to our surprise, a large native cat stepped out from the shadows and moved along the branch of a tea-tree into the last of the afternoon sun and then stood tall and proud before us. Somehow it knew we were not there to harm it, and immediately the words of Mr Rennie sprung to mind.

*I would never put such a spirited beastie in a cage...*

We stared in amazement at this magnificent animal, and then I caught a glimpse of Horty's face which had the most peaceful and fulfilled expression on it, surprising me as to how much seeing this animal would mean to her.

Allowing her gaze to leave the native cat, she gave me a warm smile, took hold of my hand and then drew me behind the she-oak fronds, kissing me with the same passion she had at the skating rink hall. I tried not to think that this may be our last kiss but couldn't get away from the feeling that no matter how hard we tried, we would soon want to be kissing others.

Quickly we returned to see Millie and Sniffle still transfixed on the bold animal, unaware of our disappearance. Horty then tugged gently on my sleeve and her eyes lit up like I had never seen them before.

She then gave me the cheekiest smile.

*It may not be our last kiss!*

I love you Horty Brown.

The End

# The Moon*beamers*

*An excerpt...*

It's never easy when you're the new partner...

GARY SEEARY

# PART ONE:
# BEACH

# CHAPTER 1

## Friday, 27th December 1996. Evening

*Here she comes clomping up the stairs. Why can't she walk around the house like a normal person does, or like her mum? Fiona always walks so lightly on her tiny feet, yet still with purpose.*

*Although, there is some comfort in knowing where Pixie is at any given moment.*

*Her brother, Zac, is a different kettle of fish, he's barely audible as he shuffles and mopes about — I wish he'd stomp occasionally.*

*No need to wonder what Pixie has in store for me this evening. It will have everything to do with the carry-on of last night.*

*Some things are best left in the realms of the unknown.*

"Michael, are you in there?" Pixie called from the top of the stairs.

"I sure am," I replied from inside the master bedroom.

"Can I come in?" Pixie asked.

"Sure," I replied positively, although wishing she'd just go back downstairs to her friends.

I *was* relaxed up until then, leaning against two large pillows on top of the firm king-sized bed I had found myself privileged to share twelve months ago; although only on a permanent basis for the past two.

In boxer shorts, I was in the process of reading the screenplay that Pixie's mum and my lover, Fiona, had adopted from the well-known bestseller, *The Money Trail*.

I timed Pixie's stomping and placed the script over my boxers as she burst into the room.

"Hi," Pixie said quickly and then turned back to close the door.

With the door firmly shut on the throbbing techno music that had recently commenced at the far end of the house, Pixie walked over and stood in front of the bed in barely a thread of a royal blue evening dress, before planting the fists she had formed on the way, firmly on her slim hips.

"Do you want to join us, Michael?" Pixie asked in an off-handed manner.

I straightened up against the pillows and smiled back at her. Pixie continued.

"We're having a little party in the family room — dancing and stuff ... You know." Pixie's eyes weren't meeting mine, so I wasn't convinced this was a genuine invitation.

"You know Lou, she's there. You like her. You said that the other day."

*I said 'she's alright' the other day.*

"Thanks, but I don't think so. I'm engrossed in your mum's script of *The Money Trail,* it's too good to put down. I'd like to finish it in one go if I could. It's much better than the book."

Pixie began to stare at the script over my boxers, which I preferred she didn't.

*Eyes up, thanks.*

"Yeah, the book was a crock of shit." Pixie said in her usual colourful manner, "I read it at school. Mum's really put a cracker up its arse — I love it."

Thankfully, Pixie's eyes then returned to my face.

"I agree. Only one thing — Too heavy on the violence." I stated.

"Come on, Michael, don't be such a pussy. Everyone loves violence," Pixie said as she pretended to stab someone with an invisible knife. "Except the people getting bashed or killed, that is."

Pixie then sat without asking at the end of the bed, below my feet. I gradually closed my legs.

"Are you going somewhere later?" I asked to make conversation, feeling she wanted to say something. "You look dressed for a night out."

"I wish I was. I wanted to see if Lou and I could get into a club in the city, but she doesn't want to go. She wants to stay here with her juvenile friggin' friends." Pixie replied with a fair degree of annoyance.

"I'm over hanging around with those Sailing Club tossers.

Might end up like Tracey."

*Don't start on her.*

Pixie pulled her long blonde hair into a ponytail and then let it go of it just as quickly. She preened its full length one time and then stopped.

"Why are you here, Michael? ... I mean, why are you still here? Mum's away and you're here. It's bullshit." Pixie said at me, and then seemed to search for pre-planned words.

"Zac and I don't feel comfortable."

*Well, that's a nice welcome into the fold — and Zac only knows comfortable.*

Pixie stood, feigned a look of supremacy and then smoothed down her dress as if I was being rude for not giving an immediate answer.

"Bad luck," I said flatly. "Your mum and I worked it out before she left. She doesn't want any big parties. Besides, I live here, too."

Pixie walked back towards the door and then spun around to face me.

"You know, Dad's barely gone and you're acting like the boss around here. You could be a sick fucker for all we know — and we're stuck with you. Who knows what you were up to last night."

"I was checking out a noise."

"Were you ... really?" Pixie asked, her eyes held wide open for emphasis. "Do you always perv on people when you're checking out a noise?"

"Would you like to talk about last night? I'm happy to."
I asked seriously, confident it was the real reason she was
here.

Pixie turned her face away dismissively, showing a lack
of maturity on her behalf. I took another tack.

"Have you spoken to Zac?" I asked, although feeling
she would have probably let that slide, seeing little sign of
the closeness with her brother that would be required to
discuss such a delicate subject.

"He's *my* brother, so what he does has nothing to do with
you." Pixie replied, trying for bitterness, but ending up
sounding like a child. She then whispered.

"I wish you'd give us some space."

"Like I said before — bad luck. And by the way, I've been
trying not to disrupt your, or Zac's, day to day life by being
here?"

"Have you...?"

Pixie walked back to the bed, her face still turned away
so she didn't have to look me in the eye.

"I asked Mum why you got divorced. She said I should
think about growing up pretty soon ... but I still wouldn't
mind knowing."

"No, that's fine. I've got nothing to hide."

*I'm shutting this down, she's crossed a line by asking about*
*something I would probably share with her in time.*

How could I explain in this room, on this bed, which
was still far from being mine, what brought an end to the

wonderful life I had, with a wonderful woman? — I rushed my words.

"Okay, it's simple. We wanted different things. That's the whole story."

I placed the script on the bed, swung around to its edge and then leant down to pick up my denim shorts.

"Alright, I'd love to come down," I said through a forced smile. "Could be a blast."

Pixie couldn't wait to respond.

"Now, you're talking shit."

My feet got tangled as I tried to pull up my shorts in rapid time; giving up in frustration, I turned to face my inquisitor.

"What do you want from me, Pixie?"

Pixie waved a finger at me in a dismissive way as if she didn't need to justify her words, or should ever have to, and then wrapped her arms over her chest.

"I just want to know if you're serious about Mum," Pixie asked perhaps never believing I was.

"Okay, I'll call my folks tomorrow and ask if they're happy to have their grown-up son back with them for a few days, then I'll see you and Zac when your mum returns. I hope that's comfortable enough for you?"

Pixie stomped back towards the door, opened it fully and then without being courteous enough to turn around to face me, said.

"Weak as piss."

I wasn't going to engage anymore. It would only turn into a slanging match. I had given her what she wanted.

"Don't forget, you'll need to walk Horry every morning now," I added firmly.

Pixie continued to stand in the doorway with her back to me, then whispered. I could just make out her words.

"I miss my dad."

She left before I had time to say, 'I love your mum.'

~

9 780648 002864